TRISTYN BARBERI

City Of Whispers

Neon Shadows Duology

First published by TB Press 2025

Copyright © 2025 by Tristyn Barberi

All rights reserved. No part of this publication may be reproduced, stored or transmitted in any form or by any means, electronic, mechanical, photocopying, recording, scanning, or otherwise without written permission from the publisher. It is illegal to copy this book, post it to a website, or distribute it by any other means without permission.

This novel is entirely a work of fiction. The names, characters and incidents portrayed in it are the work of the author's imagination. Any resemblance to actual persons, living or dead, events or localities is entirely coincidental.

First edition

*This book was professionally typeset on Reedsy.
Find out more at reedsy.com*

Contents

Chapter 1	1
Chapter 2	4
Chapter 3	7
Chapter 4	10
Chapter 5	13
Chapter 6	16
Chapter 7	19
Chapter 8	22
Chapter 9	26
Chapter 10	29
Chapter 11	32
Chapter 12	35
Chapter 13	39
Chapter 14	43
Chapter 15	47
Chapter 16	50
Chapter 17	53
Chapter 18	57
Chapter 19	60
Chapter 20	63
Chapter 21	66
Chapter 22	69
Chapter 23	73
Chapter 24	76

Chapter 25	79
Chapter 26	81
Chapter 27	84
Chapter 28	88
Chapter 29	91
Chapter 30	94
Chapter 31	97
Chapter 32	100
Chapter 33	102
Chapter 34	105
Chapter 35	109
Chapter 36	112
Chapter 37	115
Chapter 38	119
Chapter 39	123
Chapter 40	126
Chapter 41	129
Chapter 42	131
Chapter 43	134
Chapter 44	137
Chapter 45	140
About The Author	142
Also By Tristyn Barberi	143

Chapter 1

The bright, colorful signs of the Serpent's Coil district splashed their light onto the wet streets, making the narrow alleys glow with streaks of blue and green. Nineteen-year-old Anya Petrova moved quickly through the crowded area, her steps sure and steady. This sprawling, futuristic city of Veridia was her home, a place of towering, brightly lit buildings and hidden shadows, and she knew its every twist and turn.

Tonight, she was heading towards a small, glowing sign that read "Elena's Fix-It." This was her mother's small repair shop, squeezed between a noodle stand that glowed with its own light and a shop selling robots that sometimes didn't work quite right. The familiar smell of hot metal and electrical parts usually made Anya feel at home, but tonight, she was a little worried. Her mother, Elena, worked incredibly hard to support Anya and her younger brother.

When Anya opened the door, she heard the familiar sounds of tools clinking and saw the soft light over Elena's workbench. Her mother looked up, her kind eyes showing a hint of tiredness, and a small smile appeared on her face. "Anya, my sunshine. You're late getting back."

"The public transport was a mess again, Mama," Anya explained, taking off her worn jacket. "Something about the richer parts of the city needing it more." It was always the same story – the wealthy people living in the higher levels of Veridia always got what they needed first.

Ten-year-old Misha, Anya's little brother with messy brown hair and curious eyes, rushed out from behind a pile of broken machines. "Anya!" he shouted happily, grabbing her legs in a hug.

Anya smiled, finally feeling some of the tension leave her. Misha was their joy, a bright spot in their often difficult lives. He still looked up at the tall, shining buildings with wonder, not really understanding the unfairness of their society.

They lived in a single, small room above the repair shop. The walls were thin, so they could always hear the noise from the street below. Their furniture was old and fixed up by Elena – a patched couch that turned into a bed, a shaky table, and shelves full of spare parts and Misha's collection of interesting bits of technology he found. It wasn't fancy, but it was their home. It was where they shared simple meals, where Elena sang them soft songs that sometimes sounded a little sad, and where Anya dreamed of a future where Misha wouldn't have to worry about not having enough.

Looking out their window, they could see the huge, elegant buildings in the upper parts of the city reaching into the sky, their smooth surfaces shining. Fast, private vehicles flew between them like bright insects, so different from the slow, crowded public transport Anya had just used. The beautiful Zenith Tower and the important company buildings seemed like a different world, a constant reminder of the huge gap between the rich and the poor in Veridia.

"Did you get the piece for Mr. Tiberius's new eye?" Elena asked, wiping her hands on a cloth.

CHAPTER 1

Anya nodded, pulling a small, sealed container from her bag. "And I managed to get the price down a bit. It wasn't easy." Every single credit was important. Elena wasn't as healthy as she used to be, and Misha needed new shoes. Anya often felt the weight of taking care of them, which made her look serious but never lessened her fierce love for her family.

As the bright signs outside glowed even more intensely, casting long shadows in their small room, Anya watched Misha drawing amazing flying machines on an old tablet. A strong feeling grew inside her. She would do anything to protect them from the harsh realities of Veridia, from the crime and corruption that lurked even in their neighborhood. She just didn't know yet the painful price that finding the truth and fighting for what's right would demand in this dazzling but unfair world.

Chapter 2

The regulated hum of the Serpentine Sector faded behind Anya as she slipped through a gap in a perimeter fence marked with faded "Restricted Access" warnings. The air here felt different – heavier, dustier, and strangely still compared to the vibrant energy of the occupied districts. This was the Silenced Spire, a section of Veridia abandoned decades ago after a mysterious structural failure, now a skeletal finger pointing accusingly at the sky.

Curiosity, a trait Elena often gently chided, tugged at Anya. While others in the lower sectors spoke of the Silenced Spire with superstitious whispers of ghosts and unstable foundations, Anya saw only a mystery, a forgotten corner of her city ripe for exploration. Tonight, with Elena and Misha asleep in their small module, the lure of the unknown had proven too strong to resist.

Her boots crunched on loose synth-crete as she navigated the deserted avenues. Buildings loomed on either side, their once-gleaming facades now scarred and darkened. Nature, in the form of tenacious vines and hardy, mutated flora, was slowly reclaiming the artificial landscape. The silence was broken only by the whisper of the wind through shattered window panes and the occasional scuttling sound that sent a shiver down her spine.

CHAPTER 2

Anya carried a small, multi-tool and a scavenged light-rod, its beam cutting through the gloom. She wasn't aimless; rumors among the street kids spoke of salvageable tech left behind in the Spire, valuable components that could fetch a decent price. But tonight, something else propelled her – a restless feeling, a sense that Veridia held more secrets than its polished surface revealed.

She found herself drawn to a particularly imposing structure, its entrance partially collapsed but still accessible. It looked like it might have once been a research facility or a high-level corporate office. Inside, dust lay thick as a blanket, coating abandoned workstations and overturned furniture. The air smelled of decay and forgotten energy.

As Anya swept her light across a debris-strewn floor, something metallic glinted beneath a pile of shattered data-slates. She knelt down, carefully clearing away the debris. It was a small, palm-sized device, its casing made of a dark, unfamiliar alloy. Unlike the sleek, standardized tech prevalent in Veridia, this device had a raw, almost archaic feel to it.

Intrigued, Anya brushed off more of the dust. There were no visible activation buttons or ports, just smooth, seamless surfaces etched with faint, almost invisible symbols. As she turned it over in her hand, a section of the casing subtly shifted, revealing a thin, almost microscopic line of light that pulsed with a faint blue hue.

Anya held her breath. This wasn't standard salvage. This felt... different. It hummed faintly in her palm, a subtle vibration that resonated deep within her. She tried to interface with it, running basic diagnostic commands through her neural link, but the device remained stubbornly unresponsive. It was like a language she didn't understand, a piece of a puzzle she hadn't even known existed.

Suddenly, a flicker of movement in the shadows at the far end of the room caught her eye. Anya instinctively extinguished her light-rod, her heart pounding. She pressed herself against a crumbling wall, straining her ears. The sound was faint, but unmistakable – the soft crunch of footsteps on debris.

Someone else was here. In the Silenced Spire.

Fear mixed with a surge of adrenaline. This forgotten place wasn't as deserted as she thought. Clutching the mysterious device tightly in her hand, Anya melted further into the shadows, her adventurous spirit now overshadowed by a prickling sense of danger. She had stumbled upon something hidden, something valuable enough for others to risk entering this forbidden zone. And in that moment, she knew her curiosity had led her down a path that could be far more perilous than she could have ever imagined. The faint blue pulse in her hand seemed to echo the uncertain beat of her own heart, a silent promise of the conflict to come.

Chapter 3

The crunching footsteps grew closer, the sound echoing eerily in the cavernous space. Anya's breath hitched in her throat. She risked a quick glance through a crack in the crumbling wall. A figure moved with a fluid, almost predatory grace, their form obscured by the dim ambient light filtering through the broken ceiling. They carried a light-rod similar to hers, its beam systematically sweeping across the debris. They were searching.

Panic surged through Anya, cold and sharp. They must have seen her light, or perhaps they knew someone was exploring the Silenced Spire tonight. Whatever the reason, the urgency in their movements was unmistakable. She clutched the smooth, cool device tighter. It was the only thing that felt real in this suddenly hostile environment.

Moving with a speed born of desperation, Anya silently backed away from the wall. Her street instincts, honed in the crowded lower sectors, kicked in. She needed to create distance, to find an escape route. The main entrance was likely compromised. That left the shadowed recesses of the building.

She darted behind a toppled data-server, its exposed wires sparking faintly. The searching light flickered nearby. They were close. Anya held her breath, willing her heart to stop pounding so loudly in her ears.

Just as the light beam began to sweep her hiding place, Anya made her move. She scrambled behind another large piece of equipment, then sprinted low across the open floor towards a gaping hole in the far wall – a section where the building had partially collapsed. The uneven terrain made her footing treacherous, but adrenaline fueled her flight.

"Hey!" A sharp voice cut through the silence, followed by the sound of দ্রুত footsteps pounding on the synth-crete. They had seen her.

Anya didn't look back. She scrambled through the jagged opening, sharp edges tearing at her jacket. On the other side, she found herself in a narrow, overgrown alleyway, the skeletal remains of another abandoned structure looming above. The air was thick with the scent of damp earth and decaying metal.

Her pursuer was close behind, their heavier footfalls echoing in the confined space. Anya risked a glance over her shoulder. The figure was silhouetted against the dim light spilling from the building, their features still obscured, but their intent was clear. They were fast.

Anya veered sharply to the left, ducking behind a rusted-out transport drone. The alleyway was a maze of discarded junk and tangled vegetation, offering both obstacles and potential cover. She could hear her pursuer crashing through the undergrowth behind her.

She needed to lose them, and fast. The Silenced Spire was a labyrinth, and she knew its forgotten pathways better than anyone chasing her likely would. She scrambled over a pile of debris, her muscles burning, and slipped into a narrow crevice between two collapsing walls.

The sound of her pursuer's footsteps grew louder, then paused just outside her hiding place. Anya held her breath, every nerve in her body screaming. She could almost feel their presence, their gaze sweeping the area.

After what felt like an eternity, the footsteps moved on, fading slightly into the distance. But Anya knew they wouldn't give up easily. They had seen her, and they clearly wanted whatever she now possessed.

Emerging cautiously from her hiding spot, Anya knew she couldn't stay in the Silenced Spire. It was no longer a place of mystery and adventure; it was a hunting ground. She needed to get back to the relative safety of the lower sectors, back to Elena and Misha.

Clutching the strange device tightly, she began to move again, her earlier curiosity replaced by a gnawing fear. She had stumbled into something dangerous, something that had drawn unwanted attention. Her rebellious nature had led her down a path she hadn't anticipated, and now, she was running for her life, the faint blue pulse in her hand a silent reminder of the trouble she now carried. The price of her curiosity might be far higher than she ever imagined.

Chapter 4

Anya burst through the door of Elena's Fix-It, breathless and heart pounding. The familiar scent of solder and cleaning fluid usually brought comfort, but tonight it only amplified her anxiety. Elena, who had been meticulously repairing a cracked optical lens, looked up, her brow furrowing with concern. Misha, perched on a stool tinkering with a deactivated security bot, turned wide, questioning eyes towards his sister.

"Anya! What's wrong?" Elena's voice held a sharp edge of worry.

"Someone... someone was in the Silenced Spire," Anya gasped, trying to catch her breath. "They saw me. I think... I think they were after something." She didn't mention the device yet, her instincts screaming to keep it secret, at least for now.

Elena's eyes narrowed. "After what? Did they hurt you?"

"I'm okay, Mama. I got away." Anya forced a reassuring smile, not wanting to fully alarm them. "Just... shaken."

Misha, sensing the shift in the atmosphere, hopped off his stool and approached her cautiously. "What happened in the Spire, Anya? You said it was just old buildings."

"It... it wasn't empty," Anya said vaguely. "And I think someone didn't want me there." She knew she couldn't keep them completely in the dark, but she needed time to process what had happened and decide what to do with the mysterious device.

"You shouldn't go to those abandoned places, Anya," Elena said sternly, her usual gentle tone replaced with concern. "It's too dangerous."

"I know, Mama. I won't go back there," Anya promised, though a part of her knew that promise might be hard to keep. The device in her pocket felt like a heavy weight, a silent question mark hanging over their lives.

Later, after Elena had soothed a worried Misha back to sleep in their shared living module, Anya's mind raced. She couldn't just leave the device lying around. It had attracted dangerous attention, and their small living space offered little security. She needed a hiding place, somewhere unexpected, somewhere only she would think to look.

Her gaze scanned the cramped room, taking in the familiar clutter. Her eyes landed on Misha's collection of scavenged tech trinkets, a chaotic assortment of broken circuits, discarded chips, and deactivated gadgets piled in a dusty corner. It was the perfect camouflage.

Working quickly and quietly, Anya retrieved a small, non-functional audio recorder from Misha's hoard. Its casing was cracked and its internal components long gone. With careful movements, she pried open the back panel, creating a small cavity. The mysterious device fit snugly inside.

She then meticulously reassembled the recorder, making sure it looked exactly as it had before – a piece of junk among other pieces of junk. Placing it back in Misha's pile, nestled amongst other equally uninteresting items, a sliver of relief washed over her. Who would think to look for anything important in a child's collection of broken toys?

Now that the device was hidden, Anya could finally begin to think. What was it? Why were people in the Silenced Spire looking for it? And why had they chased her? She knew one thing for sure: her life, and perhaps the lives of Elena and Misha, had just become a lot more complicated. The adventure she had sought had found her, but it had arrived cloaked in danger, and the answers she needed were shrouded in shadow. For now, all she could do was wait, watch, and try to understand the strange, pulsing weight hidden amongst her brother's discarded treasures.

Chapter 5

The neon-drenched alleys of the Data Exchange district buzzed with a frenetic energy, a stark contrast to the silent decay of the Silenced Spire. Anya moved through the throngs of data-peddlers and information seekers, her senses on high alert. This was where secrets were bought and sold, where whispers could become fortunes, and where danger often lurked in the digital shadows.

She was looking for Jax, a wiry info-broker with eyes that seemed to hold the weight of a thousand forgotten databases. He operated out of a cramped booth tucked away in a less-trafficked corner of the Exchange, his reputation for discretion and access to obscure information making him a valuable, if risky, contact.

Finding his booth, marked by a flickering holographic sign of a stylized question mark, Anya approached cautiously. Jax was hunched over a glowing data-slate, his fingers flying across the interface. He looked up, his gaze sharp and assessing.

"Looking to buy or sell, kid?" His voice was a low rasp, like static clinging to a weak signal.

"Buy," Anya replied, her voice steady despite the knot of anxiety in her stomach. "Information. About unusual tech... possibly recovered from the Silenced Spire."

Jax's eyes narrowed slightly. "The Spire? That's old news,

kid. Nothing but scrap and bad memories there."

"This would be recent," Anya pressed. "Something... small, made of a dark alloy, with faint blue lights. Not standard Veridia tech."

Jax leaned back in his creaking chair, his gaze unwavering. He tapped a finger on his data-slate. "Unusual tech from the Spire... that could be worth something to the right people. Why the sudden interest?"

Anya hesitated. She couldn't reveal that she possessed the item. "Just... heard rumors. Someone might be looking for something specific that came out of there."

Jax studied her for a long moment, his silence making Anya's unease grow. He seemed to be weighing her words, calculating the potential value of her inquiry. Finally, he shrugged. "Can't say I've heard anything matching that description. The Spire isn't exactly a hot topic of conversation these days. Most folks prefer to forget it exists."

He paused, then added, "But information like that... it doesn't come cheap, even if I did have it. And asking about the Spire... that can attract the wrong kind of attention." His gaze flickered towards a discreetly placed surveillance orb in the corner of his booth.

Anya understood the unspoken warning. The Data Exchange was a place of constant monitoring. Asking the wrong questions could have consequences.

"I understand," she said, trying to sound nonchalant. "Just a dead end then." She offered a small credit chip. "For your time."

Jax took the chip, his eyes still fixed on her. "Keep your nose clean, kid. Some doors are better left unopened."

With a growing sense of frustration and unease, Anya left

Jax's booth and melted back into the crowded streets. She had hoped for a quick lead, some understanding of the strange device she now possessed. Instead, she had drawn a blank and, more worryingly, perhaps put herself on someone's radar. Jax's subtle warning about attracting the wrong attention lingered in her mind.

As she made her way back towards the familiar, if less glamorous, streets of the Serpent's Coil, Anya couldn't shake the feeling that she was being watched. She glanced over her shoulder several times, but the dense crowds offered no clear indication of pursuit. Still, a prickling sensation on the back of her neck persisted.

Unbeknownst to Anya, as she had been questioning Jax, a silent notification had flickered across his data-slate. A discreet alert, triggered by keywords related to "unusual tech" and "Silenced Spire." Jax, ever the pragmatist, had flagged her inquiry to a shadowy contact, a silent report filed without Anya ever knowing she had become a subject of interest.

Chapter 6

The familiar hum of Elena's Fix-It was absent. Instead, an unsettling silence hung in the air as Anya pushed open the workshop door. A cold dread washed over her, a stark contrast to the usual warmth and activity that greeted her. The workbench was overturned, tools scattered across the floor like fallen soldiers. A shattered data-slate lay near the entrance, its screen displaying a distorted image of Elena's face.

"Mama? Misha?" Anya's voice was a strained whisper, echoing in the sudden emptiness.

She rushed into their living module, her heart pounding a frantic rhythm against her ribs. The small space was in disarray. The modular seating unit was askew, cushions ripped. A child's drawing of a fantastical sky-tram lay crumpled on the floor. There was no sign of Elena or Misha. Just the chilling evidence of a violent struggle.

Panic clawed at Anya's throat. She frantically searched every corner, every hiding place, but they were gone. Vanished.

Tears welled in her eyes as she stumbled back into the workshop, her mind reeling. Who would do this? Why?

Her first instinct was to contact the Veridia Enforcers. Surely, they could help. But the automated system was cold and impersonal, directing her to a distant precinct. When she finally managed to speak to a live officer, his disinterest was palpable.

"Missing persons in the lower sectors are a common occurrence," the officer droned, his voice laced with bureaucratic indifference. "File a report online. We'll look into it when we have the resources."

His dismissive tone sent a fresh wave of despair crashing over Anya. They didn't care. Elena and Misha were just another statistic in the sprawling metropolis. She was alone.

Desperate, Anya sought out a few of Elena's acquaintances in the neighborhood, faces etched with hardship and suspicion. No one had seen anything, their eyes darting nervously as if afraid to get involved. The undercurrents of fear in the Serpent's Coil ran deep.

As Anya stood numbly in the street outside her ransacked home, a hunched figure emerged from the shadows of a nearby alley. It was Old Man Tiberius, the recipient of Elena's repaired ocular implant, his cybernetic eye gleaming faintly in the dim light. He was a recluse, a man who seemed to exist on the fringes of society, observing everything but rarely interacting.

He shuffled closer, his gaze surprisingly sharp despite his age. "They took them," he rasped, his voice like dry leaves rustling.

"Who? Who took my family?" Anya pleaded, grabbing his arm.

Tiberius's grip tightened on her hand, his cybernetic fingers surprisingly strong. "The ones who whisper in the network's veins. The ones who don't like questions." His gaze flickered towards the upper levels of the city. "You stirred something, child. Something they wanted kept buried."

Anya's blood ran cold. Jax's warning about attracting the wrong attention echoed in her mind. Had her inquiry about the Silenced Spire somehow led to this?

"You need to be careful," Tiberius continued, his voice dropping to a near whisper. "They have eyes everywhere. Trust no one in the light." He released her hand abruptly. "Look to the shadows for answers. Sometimes, the forgotten remember more than the privileged."

Before Anya could press him for more information, Tiberius melted back into the darkness, leaving her standing alone in the cold night, his cryptic words hanging heavy in the air. The authorities were useless, her neighbors fearful. Her only lead was the unsettling pronouncement of an old recluse, a warning to trust the shadows and a chilling confirmation that her actions had somehow put her family in grave danger. Desperation gnawed at her, but beneath it, a fierce resolve began to harden. She would find Elena and Misha, no matter the cost. She would navigate the shadows if that's where the answers lay.

Chapter 7

Anya became a ghost in the underbelly of Veridia, a shadow moving through the dimly lit corridors and forgotten corners the Enforcers ignored. Sleep became a luxury she could barely afford, fueled by cheap synth-coffee and a desperate need for answers. She revisited Jax's booth, but the info-broker feigned ignorance, his eyes darting nervously as if he regretted their previous interaction. Other contacts she knew, small-time hustlers and data scavengers, offered nothing but shrugs and fearful glances. The disappearance of Elena and Misha had seemingly vanished into the city's vast indifference.

Days bled into nights, each one a frustrating cycle of dead ends and mounting despair. The Enforcers' online report remained untouched, another forgotten file in their digital archives. Anya felt the walls of Veridia closing in on her, the glittering towers mocking her helplessness. Tiberius's words echoed in her mind: "Trust no one in the light." He had been right. The official channels were useless, perhaps even complicit.

She started frequenting the more clandestine gathering spots – the illicit tech markets that sprung up in abandoned subway tunnels, the underground gambling dens where secrets were traded like currency, the dimly lit synth-ale bars where the dispossessed sought solace. She listened intently to every hushed conversation, every drunken boast, every whispered rumor. She showed faded holograms of Elena and Misha, her voice tight with a forced calm that belied the turmoil within.

Most people offered empty condolences or shook their heads, unwilling to get involved. The fear of those "who whisper in the network's veins" seemed pervasive. Anya began to feel a crushing loneliness, the weight of her isolation almost unbearable.

Then, one rain-slicked evening in a dimly lit bar in the Serpent's Coil, she overheard a fragment of a conversation. Two figures huddled in a corner booth, their voices low and urgent.

"...they disappear people, just like that. No trace. Especially if they stumble onto something they shouldn't..."

"...heard of... the Network? They say they operate outside the system, help those the city forgets..."

Anya's ears perked up. The Network. She had heard whispers of them before – a shadowy collective, rumored to be skilled in infiltration and information gathering, a group that worked outside the established order, helping those who had nowhere else to turn. They were spoken of in hushed tones, their existence more legend than fact.

As the two figures in the booth prepared to leave, Anya took a deep breath and approached them. "Excuse me," she said, her voice trembling slightly. "I couldn't help but overhear... you mentioned the Network?"

The two figures froze, their eyes instantly wary. One, a woman with intricate cybernetic tattoos tracing patterns across her face, regarded Anya with suspicion. The other, a hulking man with a shaved head and piercing gaze, remained silent, his posture radiating caution.

"That's not a name you should be throwing around, kid," the

woman said, her voice low and gravelly.

"I... I need help," Anya pleaded, her carefully constructed composure finally cracking. "My mother and brother... they were taken. The authorities won't do anything. Someone mentioned... the Network might be able to help people like me."

The woman exchanged a look with her companion. After a long, tense silence, she spoke again, her tone softening slightly. "The Network doesn't just help anyone, kid. They help those who are truly abandoned by the system. What makes you think they'd help you?"

Anya's voice broke as she recounted the chaos in her home, the Enforcers' indifference, Tiberius's cryptic warning about those who didn't like questions. She didn't mention the device, still wary of revealing too much to strangers.

The woman listened intently, her expression unreadable. Finally, she nodded slowly. "There are whispers... ways to reach them. But it's dangerous. And there are no guarantees." She reached into a pocket and produced a small, unmarked data-chip. "Be at the Crimson Lantern market in the Foundry District at midnight, three nights from now. Ask for 'Silas.' Tell him you were sent by 'Whisper.'"

Anya's heart leaped with a flicker of hope. A lead. A chance. "Thank you," she whispered, clutching the data-chip like a lifeline.

The woman gave a curt nod. "Don't mention our names. Don't tell anyone about this. And be careful who you trust. In this city, shadows have ears." With that, she and her companion disappeared back into the crowded bar, leaving Anya standing alone once more, but this time, with a fragile thread of hope to cling to in the overwhelming darkness. The Network. It was a long shot, but it was the only shot she had left.

Chapter 8

The Crimson Lantern market in the Foundry District was a chaotic swirl of flickering neon signs, the sizzle of street food vendors, and the murmur of illicit deals conducted in hushed tones. The air hung thick with the smell of ozone, synthetic spices, and desperation. Anya, clutching the data-chip like a fragile promise, navigated the crowded stalls, her senses on high alert. Midnight was fast approaching.

She scanned the faces in the throng, searching for anyone who looked like they might know more than they let on. Finally, she spotted a lone figure leaning against a grimy pillar, his face obscured by the shadow of a wide-brimmed hat. He exuded an air of quiet watchfulness that set him apart from the surrounding chaos. Taking a deep breath, Anya approached him.

"Silas?" she asked, her voice barely above a whisper.

The figure slowly lifted his head, his eyes, when they met hers, were sharp and assessing. "Who's asking?" His voice was low, a gravelly rumble that seemed to vibrate in the damp night air.

"I was sent by... Whisper," Anya replied, the code word feeling strange and significant on her tongue.

Silas studied her intently for a long moment, his gaze unwavering. Anya felt a wave of nervous anticipation wash over her.

This was it. Her only lead.

Finally, he spoke, his tone flat and devoid of emotion. "Whisper sends a lot of lost souls my way. What makes your plight so different?"

Anya poured out her story, the words tumbling out in a rush of desperation – the disappearance of Elena and Misha, the Enforcers' indifference, Tiberius's cryptic warning. She spoke of her fear and her unwavering determination to find her family. She didn't mention the device, still unsure of who she could truly trust.

Silas listened in silence, his expression unreadable. When she finished, he remained quiet for a long moment, the sounds of the market swirling around them.

Then, he delivered the blow. "I can't help you."

Anya's heart sank. The fragile hope she had been clinging to shattered into a million pieces. "But... Whisper said you could help those the system forgets," she stammered, her voice thick with despair.

Silas's gaze remained steady. "The Network has its own priorities. We don't take on every lost cause that stumbles through the shadows. Your situation... it sounds personal. We deal with systemic issues, with the larger injustices that plague Veridia."

"But my family *is* a systemic issue!" Anya argued, her voice rising in desperation. "They were taken, and no one cares because we live in the lower sectors! Isn't that the kind of injustice you fight?"

Silas remained unmoved. "Perhaps. But we need more than just a heartbroken daughter's plea. We need evidence, we need a connection to something larger. Right now, all you have is a story." He turned to leave. "Find something more concrete, something that ties into the bigger picture, and maybe... maybe then we can talk."

Anya stood frozen, the noise of the market blurring around her. He was dismissing her, turning his back on her only chance. The weight of her helplessness crashed down on her, heavy and suffocating. Tears welled in her eyes, blurring the already chaotic lights of the market.

She watched Silas disappear into the crowd, her shoulders slumping in defeat. The journey to the Foundry District, the fragile hope, had all been for nothing. She was back where she started, alone and without answers.

The walk back to the Serpent's Coil was a blur of pain and despair. The vibrant city lights seemed to mock her sorrow. When she finally reached the relative quiet of her ransacked home, the emptiness of it hit her with renewed force. Elena's absence was a gaping hole in the silence, Misha's missing laughter a phantom echo in the dust-filled air.

Anya sank onto the edge of their overturned seating unit, the weight of her grief threatening to overwhelm her. For a moment, she considered giving up. The task of finding her family felt impossible, the forces arrayed against her too powerful.

But then, a spark of defiance flickered within her. She thought of Elena's unwavering strength, of Misha's bright, hopeful eyes. She remembered Tiberius's cryptic words: "Look to the shadows for answers." Silas had dismissed her plea, but his words echoed in her mind: "Find something more concrete... something that ties into the bigger picture."

Anya clenched her fists, her jaw set with grim determination. Silas might have refused her for now, but she wouldn't give up. She would find that "something more." She would delve deeper into the shadows, uncover the truth behind her family's disappearance, and she would make the Network – and anyone else who stood in her way – listen. The heartbreak fueled a new kind of resolve, a burning promise that she would not rest until Elena and Misha were found.

Unseen by Anya, in the shadows of a nearby building, Silas watched her retreating figure. A flicker of something that might have been respect crossed his hardened features. He had seen the despair in her eyes, but also the stubborn refusal to be broken. The Network didn't offer help easily. Sometimes, the first test was the willingness to keep fighting even when all hope seemed lost. Anya Petrova, he suspected, was just beginning her real trial.

Chapter 9

Back in the oppressive silence of her ransacked living module, the weight of Silas's rejection pressed down on Anya. The Crimson Lantern market, her last beacon of hope, had extinguished, leaving her adrift in a sea of despair. But as she sat amidst the remnants of her former life, a flicker of memory sparked in the darkness. The device. The strange piece of tech she had found in the Silenced Spire.

In her desperation to find her family, she had almost forgotten it, stashed away amongst Misha's discarded toys. Now, Silas's words echoed in her mind: "Find something more concrete... something that ties into the bigger picture." Could the device be that something? It had felt important, different. The people who chased her in the Spire certainly seemed to think so.

Driven by a renewed sense of purpose, Anya carefully retrieved the audio recorder from Misha's collection. Her fingers fumbled slightly as she opened the hidden compartment, revealing the smooth, dark alloy of the device, its faint blue light still pulsing steadily.

She held it in her palm, turning it over and over. The etched symbols on its surface remained stubbornly unfamiliar. It didn't interface with any Veridia tech she knew. It was an enigma, a silent witness to something unknown.

CHAPTER 9

Anya knew she needed to understand what it was, where it came from, and why it seemed so important. Her limited knowledge of advanced technology wouldn't be enough. She needed help, but Silas had made it clear that the Network wasn't interested in a simple missing persons case. The device had to be the key, the connection to something larger.

Her thoughts turned to the few people in Veridia who might possess the expertise to identify such an unusual piece of tech. Most of them would be in the upper sectors, inaccessible to her. But there was one, a fringe tech-whisperer known as Glitch, who operated in the shadowy edges of the Data Exchange, dealing in black market hardware and forgotten schematics. He was eccentric and untrustworthy, but he had a reputation for understanding things others couldn't.

Knowing the risks, Anya decided it was her only option. She carefully concealed the device and prepared to venture back into the treacherous currents of the Data Exchange.

Unseen, in the labyrinthine network of surveillance feeds that crisscrossed the Serpent's Coil, Silas watched. His gaze, relayed through a discreetly placed micro-drone, followed Anya as she moved with a newfound urgency. He had dismissed her initial plea, wanting to gauge her resilience, her ability to think beyond her immediate grief. He needed to see if she possessed the tenacity and resourcefulness that the Network valued.

He observed her return to her ransacked home, the brief moment of despair that clouded her features, and then the subtle shift in her demeanor. He saw her retrieve something from a hidden location. His interest piqued. What had the grieving girl found that had reignited her determination?

As Anya slipped back into the crowded streets, heading towards the Data Exchange, Silas activated a secure comm-channel. "Keep an eye on Petrova," he murmured to an unseen contact. "She has something... something that might be more significant than we initially thought. Let's see where it leads her." He leaned back in his concealed observation post, his expression unreadable. The test was far from over. Anya's resolve was evident, but the true nature of what she carried, and the dangers it attracted, remained to be seen.

Chapter 10

Driven by the need to understand the device, Anya headed back into the chaotic sprawl of the Data Exchange. She needed access to a secure terminal, one powerful enough to analyze the unfamiliar tech. She knew of a less-than-reputable data broker named Kaelen, who boasted access to restricted search engines for a hefty price. He operated out of a heavily shielded booth near the Exchange's volatile periphery.

She found Kaelen, a gaunt man with twitchy eyes and fingers stained with synth-ink, guarding his terminal like a prized possession. "Looking for something... specific?" he asked, his gaze sharp and suspicious.

"Restricted data," Anya stated, keeping her voice low. "Something... off-network. I need to see what this is connected to." She subtly gestured to the concealed device.

Kaelen's eyes narrowed. "Off-network searches require bypass codes. Expensive ones. And if you're poking around in the wrong places..." He trailed off, a hint of threat in his tone.

Anya met his gaze. "I understand the risks. I'll pay your price." She slid a data-chip loaded with a significant portion of her dwindling credits across the counter.

Kaelen snatched it up, his eyes flicking back to Anya with a flicker of greed. "Alright. But you get five minutes. And if anyone comes sniffing around, you never saw me." He gestured to the heavily encrypted terminal. "Log in. The bypass protocols are... sensitive."

Anya sat down, her heart pounding. The login screen demanded a complex sequence of encrypted passwords and biometric scans. She fumbled with the interface, her limited hacking skills proving useless against the robust security. Just as Kaelen was about to pull the plug, a faint blue light pulsed from the device in her hand. Simultaneously, the login prompts on the screen flickered and vanished, replaced by a single, stark command line: ACCESS GRANTED.

Anya stared in disbelief. The device had somehow bypassed the seemingly impenetrable security. Before she could fully process what had happened, a new window opened, displaying encrypted files and network schematics she couldn't immediately decipher. Then, a red alert flashed on the screen, accompanied by a piercing siren that echoed through Kaelen's booth.

"Unauthorized intrusion detected on secure network," a synthesized voice blared from the terminal. "User location identified. Lockdown initiated."

Kaelen's eyes widened in panic. "Enforcers! Get out! Now! You've fried my whole setup!"

Anya ripped the device from the terminal, her mind racing. It wasn't just a key; it was a skeleton key, capable of unlocking secrets she couldn't have imagined. But now, the digital alarm had become a real one.

As she scrambled to her feet, the shielded door to Kaelen's booth burst open, revealing two figures in black tactical gear, their energy weapons charged. Veridia Enforcers. They had pinpointed her location with terrifying speed.

CHAPTER 10

"Freeze! Veridia Enforcer. Drop what you're holding and surrender!"

Anya was trapped. Kaelen had already vanished through a hidden exit. She was facing armed officers, the mysterious device glowing faintly in her hand like a beacon.

Suddenly, a section of the booth's wall shimmered and dissolved, revealing a figure cloaked in shadow, their movements swift and silent. A stun blast arced from their hand, incapacitating one of the Enforcers.

"This way," a low voice commanded, grabbing Anya's arm and pulling her through the newly created opening.

Before Anya could fully register what was happening, she was being dragged through a hidden passage, the sounds of shouting and energy fire echoing behind them. Her rescuer moved with an uncanny agility, navigating the secret pathways beneath the Data Exchange.

As they emerged into a dimly lit service tunnel, Anya finally managed to speak. "Who... who are you?"

The cloaked figure didn't answer immediately, their focus on ensuring their escape. But as they moved deeper into the underbelly of the Exchange, the realization dawned on Anya: the Network hadn't completely dismissed her after all. Someone had been watching. And they had just saved her life. The device, it seemed, had spoken a language that even the shadows understood.

Chapter 11

The cloaked figure moved with a practiced silence through the labyrinthine service tunnels, their grip on Anya's arm firm but not unkind. They navigated a world of dripping pipes, flickering emergency lights, and the low hum of Veridia's underbelly, a stark contrast to the glittering cityscape above. Finally, they reached a reinforced door, which hissed open to reveal a small, sparsely furnished room.

Once inside, the cloaked figure turned, and with a fluid motion, lowered their hood. Anya gasped. It was the woman from the bar, the one who had given her the data-chip, her face still marked by the intricate cybernetic tattoos that traced patterns across her skin.

"You move fast, 'Whisper'," Anya said, a mixture of relief and confusion swirling within her.

The woman – Whisper, apparently – gave a curt nod. "Survival in Veridia requires a certain... efficiency. You triggered a city-wide alert back there. You have something they don't want you to have." She gestured to the device Anya still clutched tightly.

"It... it bypassed their security," Anya stammered, still trying to process the rapid turn of events. "I don't understand how."

"That's a question for later," Whisper said, her gaze sharp.

CHAPTER 11

"Right now, you need to understand the kind of world you've stumbled into. Veridia isn't all gleaming towers and technological marvels. Beneath the surface, there's a rot that the privileged prefer to ignore."

She leaned against a metal table, her arms crossed. "There are those who operate completely outside the law, preying on the vulnerable. Slavery rings that snatch people from the lower sectors, their identities wiped, their lives repurposed for the whims of the elite. Organ harvesting operations that treat the poor as spare parts. And then there's the information trade, where secrets are currency, and lives can be ruined with a whisper."

Anya's blood ran cold. She had always known life in the Serpent's Coil was hard, but the casual brutality Whisper described was horrifying.

"The Enforcers you encountered?" Whisper continued, her voice grim. "Sometimes they're the law. Sometimes... they're just another arm of the powerful, protecting their interests, turning a blind eye to the darkness."

"And the people who took my family?" Anya asked, her voice trembling. "Do you know who they were?"

Whisper's expression turned thoughtful. "Not definitively. But the speed and efficiency of their response, and their intense interest in that device... it suggests a highly organized group with significant resources. They operate in the shadows, and they don't like loose ends. The fact that they moved so quickly after you accessed the network points to a sophisticated surveillance system and a ruthless efficiency."

"So... they took Elena and Misha because of this?" Anya held up the device.

"It's the most likely explanation," Whisper confirmed. "That device… it's a key to something they want to keep hidden. Your unauthorized access triggered alarms they can't ignore. And anyone connected to that intrusion becomes a liability."

A wave of guilt washed over Anya. Her curiosity, her desperate search for answers, had put her family in even greater danger.

"Why are you helping me?" Anya asked, her voice raw with emotion. "You don't even know me."

Whisper's gaze was steady. "The Network doesn't stand idly by while the powerful prey on the weak. And sometimes," a hint of a smile touched her lips, "a spark of defiance in a desperate soul is worth investing in. You showed resourcefulness, kid. You didn't give up when Silas turned you away. That counts for something."

She looked directly at Anya, her cybernetic eyes gleaming. "But this is just the beginning. Finding out who took your family, and getting them back, won't be easy. There are forces at play here you can't even imagine. Are you ready for that?"

Anya looked down at the device in her hand, then back at Whisper. Fear still gnawed at her, but beneath it, a fierce determination burned. She had to get Elena and Misha back. No matter the cost.

"Yes," she said, her voice firm. "Tell me what I need to do."

The glittering facade of Veridia had shattered, revealing a dark and dangerous reality. But Anya Petrova was no longer just a street kid trying to survive. She was a woman with nothing left to lose, and she was ready to fight.

Chapter 12

"Vengeance is a heavy burden, Anya," Whisper said, her voice low and serious as they sat in the dimly lit safehouse. "It can consume you, leave you hollow. But it can also be a powerful motivator."

Anya's fists clenched. The image of her ransacked home, the chilling silence where Elena's gentle voice and Misha's laughter used to be, fueled a burning desire for retribution against whoever had taken them. "I want them back," she said, her voice tight with emotion. "And whoever did this... they need to pay."

"The Network can offer you the means to find your family," Whisper continued, her gaze unwavering. "We have access to information, to resources the Enforcers can only dream of. We can teach you skills you never knew you possessed – how to move unseen, how to extract information, how to defend yourself in a world that preys on the weak."

Anya's heart quickened. This was the opportunity she desperately needed. But she sensed a catch. "What's the price?"

Whisper's expression hardened. "Loyalty. Unquestioning obedience. And a willingness to do what needs to be done, even if it goes against what you believe. The Network operates in the shadows for a reason. We don't always play by the rules of the surface world. The lines between justice and vengeance can blur quickly down here."

Anya hesitated. The idea of blindly following orders, of potentially compromising her own moral compass, was unsettling. But the thought of Elena and Misha, alone and vulnerable, outweighed her reservations. "What kind of things?" she asked, her voice barely a whisper.

"Sometimes, it involves eliminating threats before they can harm others," Whisper said, her gaze direct. "Sometimes, it means making difficult choices for the greater good, as we see it. The path to finding your family may lead you down dark roads, Anya. Are you prepared to walk them?"

Anya looked down at her hands, her mind a whirlwind of conflicting emotions. The price was steep, terrifying even. But what choice did she have? The authorities had abandoned her. The Network was her only hope. "Yes," she said finally, her voice filled with a grim resolve. "I'll do whatever it takes."

The training began the next cycle. It was brutal and relentless, pushing Anya beyond her physical and mental limits. Whisper and other members of the Network, their faces often masked or obscured, became her instructors. They taught her the art of stealth, how to move through the city's underbelly without being seen, how to pick locks and bypass security systems. They honed her reflexes, teaching her hand-to-hand combat techniques that were vicious and effective. They drilled her in information gathering, showing her how to read people, how to exploit vulnerabilities, how to extract secrets from the digital ether.

Sleep became a fleeting memory, replaced by endless drills and simulations. Every failure was met with harsh criticism, every success with a grudging nod of approval. Anya's body

CHAPTER 12

ached constantly, her knuckles were bruised, and her mind felt overloaded with new information. But with every grueling session, a new layer of resilience formed within her. The fear and helplessness she had felt after her family's disappearance began to be replaced by a steely determination.

Weeks blurred into a relentless cycle of training. Anya learned to trust her instincts, to rely on her wits, and to embrace the shadows. She was no longer just a street kid; she was becoming something else, something sharper, more dangerous.

Then, one evening, Whisper approached her, her expression unreadable. "Your initial training is complete, Anya. It's time for your first task."

Anya's breath caught in her throat. This was it. The first step on the path to finding her family.

Whisper handed her a datapad. "This is Elias Thorne. He's a local merchant in the Upper Rings. He deals in... sensitive goods. We have reason to believe he has connections to the kind of people who might be involved in disappearances like your mother's and brother's."

Anya's fingers tightened on the datapad, her heart pounding. A merchant in the opulent upper levels. It felt like a world away from the grime of the Serpent's Coil.

"Your mission is simple," Whisper continued, her voice cold and devoid of emotion. "Infiltrate his residence, gather any information you can find about his contacts and activities. If he resists... eliminate him."

Anya's blood ran cold. Eliminate him? This wasn't just about finding information. This was about taking a life. The weight of the Network's price suddenly felt crushing.

"Is this... necessary?" Anya asked, her voice barely a whisper.

Whisper's gaze was unwavering. "The people we deal with

don't respond to polite inquiries, Anya. Sometimes, the only language they understand is silence. This is the path you chose. Are you ready to walk it?"

Anya stared at Thorne's face on the datapad, a seemingly ordinary man with a smug expression. The thought of taking his life filled her with revulsion. But then she pictured Elena's worried eyes and Misha's hopeful smile. The burning desire for vengeance, for answers, flared anew.

"Yes," she said, her voice hoarse but firm. "I'm ready." The steep price of the Network's help had just become terrifyingly real. Her first mission had been offered, and it was stained with the potential for blood.

Chapter 13

Thorne's residence was a stark contrast to the cramped confines Anya was used to. It was a multi-level penthouse in the Upper Rings, all sleek chrome, panoramic windows displaying the glittering cityscape, and an oppressive sense of sterile wealth. Infiltrating it had been surprisingly easy, thanks to the Network's training and a deactivated security drone Whisper had provided.

Anya moved through the opulent rooms like a ghost, her senses on high alert. She bypassed laser grids and pressure plates with a newfound grace, her heart pounding a steady rhythm of focused intent. She searched Thorne's study, a vast space filled with expensive artifacts and holographic displays, but found nothing of immediate value. His personal data-terminals were heavily encrypted, beyond her current capabilities to crack quickly and quietly.

She moved to the next level, exploring what appeared to be living quarters. Everything spoke of extravagant comfort, yet there was an underlying coldness, an absence of genuine warmth. Drawers filled with designer clothing, automated refreshment units, and virtual art installations yielded no clues about Thorne's darker dealings.

Just as a wave of frustration began to wash over her, she heard the distinct hum of a high-end hovercar approaching outside. The soft whoosh of its descent and the gentle thud of landing echoed through the otherwise silent apartment. Someone was arriving. And it was likely Thorne himself.

Panic flared. Anya needed to find a hiding place, and fast. Her eyes darted around the room, settling on a large, ornately carved wardrobe in the corner. It was a risk – a cliché even – but it was her only immediate option. She slipped inside, the heavy doors closing behind her, plunging her into near darkness. The scent of expensive fabric and a faint, metallic tang filled the confined space.

Peeking through a narrow gap in the wardrobe doors, Anya could see the entrance to the room. The door slid open with a soft hiss, and Elias Thorne entered. He was a portly man with slicked-back hair and a self-satisfied air, just as his image on the datapad had shown. He carried a briefcase and spoke into a comm-implant, his voice smooth and condescending.

"Yes, the delivery arrived on schedule. Excellent. Ensure the stabilization protocols are initiated immediately. The client is... impatient."

His words sent a shiver down Anya's spine. Delivery? Stabilization protocols? It sounded disturbingly clinical.

Thorne moved towards a section of the wall Anya hadn't noticed before. With a touch, a seamless panel slid open, revealing a hidden room. The air that wafted out was cold and carried a faint, sickly sweet odor. Curiosity overriding her fear, Anya widened the gap in the wardrobe doors, straining to see inside.

The hidden room was dimly lit, but what Anya saw made her stomach churn. Suspended in clear, nutrient-rich tanks were various human organs – a lung, a kidney, an eye. They were preserved, almost pristine, and tagged with digital identifiers. Along one wall were shelves lined with what looked like cybernetic enhancements, polished and ready for implantation.

As Anya's horrified gaze swept across the room, she noticed a series of data-slates on a nearby console. One was open, displaying a holographic image of a young woman, her face pale and lifeless. The accompanying text detailed a "harvesting procedure" and listed various "viable components." Another slate contained a ledger of transactions, detailing large sums of credits exchanged for "donor organs" and "replacement limbs."

The metallic tang Anya had smelled in the wardrobe suddenly made sickening sense. This wasn't just a merchant dealing in sensitive goods. Elias Thorne was a trafficker in human body parts, likely sourced from victims who had "disappeared" – people like her mother and brother. The chilling realization hit Anya with the force of a physical blow. This was the darkness Whisper had spoken of, the rot beneath Veridia's glittering surface. And Thorne was right in the middle of it.

A wave of nausea and rage washed over Anya. This opulent penthouse wasn't just a home; it was a charnel house, built on the stolen lives and suffering of others. The pieces were starting to fall into place, painting a horrifying picture of the forces that might have taken her family. The "specialized acquisitions" Whisper had hinted at suddenly took on a terrifyingly literal meaning.

Her mission had changed. It was no longer just about gathering information. It was about uncovering the truth behind this monstrous operation and finding any clue that might lead her to Elena and Misha. And Elias Thorne, the smug merchant, was now more than just a target. He was a key to a nightmare Anya had only just begun to comprehend.

Chapter 14

The horror of Thorne's hidden chamber solidified Anya's resolve. This wasn't just about information anymore; it was about justice for the countless victims, and potentially for her own family. Moving with a grim determination, she carefully extracted a small optical chip recorder from her jacket, a piece of Network tech designed for silent surveillance.

Keeping low and moving with the stealth she had been taught, Anya positioned herself for clear shots of the organ tanks, the data-slates detailing the harvesting procedures, and the ledger of illicit transactions. The soft clicks of the optical chip were almost imperceptible in the sterile environment. She documented everything, the lifeless faces in the files, the chillingly clinical descriptions, the exorbitant prices paid for human components. This was the concrete evidence Silas had demanded, a glimpse into the festering wound beneath Veridia's polished exterior.

As she was about to retreat back into the wardrobe, a floorboard creaked behind her. Anya froze, every muscle tense. Thorne was still in the apartment. She had been too focused on the hidden room and hadn't heard him move.

Before she could react, Thorne's voice, now devoid of its earlier smugness, cut through the silence. "Who's there?"

Anya knew she had been compromised. Hiding was no longer an option. She had seen too much. With a deep breath, she stepped out of the shadows, the small optical chip concealed in her hand.

Thorne recoiled in surprise, his eyes widening in disbelief. "What in the blazes... who are you? How did you get in here?"

Anya's voice was cold, devoid of emotion. "I know what you're doing, Thorne. I've seen your little collection." She gestured towards the hidden room.

A flicker of fear crossed Thorne's face, quickly replaced by a mask of anger. "You have no idea what you're talking about. Get out of my home before I call the Enforcers."

"The Enforcers?" Anya scoffed. "Somehow, I doubt they'd be too surprised by your... business practices." She took a step closer, her gaze unwavering. "Tell me who you're working with. Who are your suppliers? Who are your clients?"

Thorne's hand darted towards his comm-implant. "Security! Intruder in the penthouse!"

Anya knew she had to act fast. The Network's training kicked in, her movements swift and decisive. Before Thorne could activate his comm, she lunged, her hand striking his wrist with a sharp, disabling blow. He cried out in pain, his hand flying away from his ear.

"You're not calling anyone," Anya hissed, her voice low and dangerous. "Now, answer my questions. Who took my family?"

Thorne's eyes narrowed with a mixture of fear and fury. "I don't know anything about your family, you little street rat! You've made a big mistake coming here." He lunged at her, his surprisingly strong hands reaching out.

Anya sidestepped his clumsy attack with ease, her training taking over. She delivered a sharp kick to his knee, sending him stumbling. Before he could recover, she used his momentum to throw him off balance, sending him crashing into a nearby display case filled with expensive figurines. The glass shattered, and Thorne landed heavily on the sharp fragments.

He groaned in pain, blood seeping from cuts on his arms and face. Anya stood over him, her expression grim. She hadn't wanted this, but he had forced her hand.

"Tell me," she repeated, her voice firm. "Who are you working with? Who is taking people?"

Thorne glared up at her, his face contorted with rage. "You'll regret this. They'll find you."

Anya knew he wouldn't talk willingly. The Network's lessons on extracting information echoed in her mind, but the thought of torture repulsed her. Time was running out; the Enforcers would be on their way.

With a heavy heart, Anya made a decision. Thorne was a monster, profiting from the suffering of others. He was a link in a chain that might have ensnared her family. She couldn't let him alert his contacts or escape justice.

Moving quickly, she retrieved a discarded shard of glass from the shattered display case. Thorne saw the glint in her eyes and his fear intensified. He tried to scramble away, but his injuries hampered his movement.

In a swift, brutal motion, Anya ended his life. The silence that followed was deafening, broken only by her ragged breathing. She had crossed a line, a point of no return.

Knowing the Enforcers would be swarming the penthouse soon, Anya moved quickly. She grabbed a secure data-drive from Thorne's desk, hoping it contained more information, and retraced her steps, utilizing the escape routes the Network had drilled into her. Leaving Thorne's lifeless body amidst the wreckage of his opulent life, Anya vanished back into the shadows of the Upper Rings, the weight of her actions heavy on her soul, but the burning need to find her family still her guiding star. She had evidence, and she had blood on her hands. The game had just become much more dangerous.

Chapter 15

Anya returned to the safehouse, the weight of her actions a cold knot in her stomach. Whisper met her at the entrance, her expression unreadable. Anya wordlessly handed over the optical chip and the data-drive she had taken from Thorne's penthouse.

Whisper connected the devices to a secure terminal. As the data streamed across the screen, her eyes widened slightly. The optical chip contained irrefutable evidence of Thorne's operation: the preserved organs, the harvesting logs, the ledger of transactions. The data-drive, however, revealed something far more extensive and disturbing.

"This... this is bigger than we thought," Whisper said, her voice low and grim as lines of names, encrypted financial records, and secure communications scrolled across the display. "Thorne wasn't just a lone operator. He was part of a network... a vast network that reaches into the highest levels of Veridia society."

Anya leaned closer, her breath catching in her throat as she saw familiar surnames – names associated with powerful corporations and influential families in the Upper and Middle Rings. The ledger detailed not just the sale of organs and cybernetic components, but also the acquisition of "donors" – individuals who had seemingly vanished without a trace.

"They're everywhere," Anya whispered, a chilling realization dawning on her. The indifference of the Enforcers, the fear in the eyes of the lower sector inhabitants – it all made a horrifying kind of sense now. This wasn't just a few isolated incidents; it was a deeply entrenched, systemic evil.

Over the next few weeks, Anya immersed herself even deeper in the Network's training. The revelation of the widespread corruption fueled her determination, even as the weight of what she had done haunted her. She pushed herself harder, her movements becoming sharper, her understanding of the city's undercurrents more profound.

She also began to interact more with other members of the Network. They were a diverse group, united by a shared sense of having been failed or betrayed by the system. There was Lynx, a master of infiltration with an uncanny ability to blend into any environment. There was Ronan, a hulking former security specialist with a knack for demolitions and heavy weaponry. And there was Cipher, a brilliant hacker who could unravel the most complex digital fortresses.

Anya learned from each of them, absorbing their skills and their perspectives. She heard their stories – tales of injustice, of families torn apart, of the powerful exploiting the vulnerable. These conversations solidified her understanding of the Network's purpose, their willingness to operate outside the law to fight a deeper corruption.

One evening, she sat with Silas in a quiet corner of the safehouse. He regarded her with a newfound respect in his usually impassive gaze. "You acted decisively, Anya. Thorne is no longer a threat. But you also crossed a threshold. Are you prepared for the consequences?"

Anya met his gaze steadily. "I did what I had to do. He was

involved in something monstrous. And if that's what it takes to find my family and expose this... then yes, I'm prepared."

Silas nodded slowly. "The path ahead will be fraught with danger. The people involved in this network are powerful and ruthless. But you are no longer alone. The evidence you recovered has given us a significant advantage. We now know the scope of their operation."

Cipher, hunched over a holographic display nearby, interjected, "We've been able to cross-reference some of the names on Thorne's ledger with missing persons reports – the ones the Enforcers conveniently ignored. The connections are undeniable. They're targeting people from the lower sectors, those who won't be missed."

Anya's heart clenched. Elena and Misha... were they among those names? The thought sent a fresh wave of fear through her, but it also strengthened her resolve.

"What now?" she asked, her voice firm.

Whisper stepped forward, her cybernetic eyes gleaming with determination. "Now, Anya, we dismantle their network, piece by piece. We expose their crimes to the light. And we find your family." She laid a hand on Anya's shoulder. "You're one of us now. And we don't leave our own behind."

The weight of her actions remained, a shadow clinging to Anya. But it was now accompanied by a sense of belonging, a shared purpose, and a burning hope that she was finally on the right path. The fight for justice, and for her family, had just begun.

Chapter 16

The safehouse became Anya's crucible. Sleep was a snatched luxury between grueling training sessions that pushed her body and mind to their breaking point. The Network's methods were brutal, efficient, and tailored to survival in the shadows of Veridia.

Lynx, a woman whose movements were as silent and fluid as her namesake, took charge of Anya's physical conditioning. The training began before dawn, with punishing runs through the deserted service tunnels, her lungs burning with each ragged breath. She learned to navigate treacherous rooftops, leaping across gaping chasms with a fear she fought to suppress. Lynx taught her the art of free-climbing, her fingers raw and bleeding as she scaled sheer walls, the city lights a dizzying expanse below.

Combat was visceral and unforgiving. Ronan, his massive frame a testament to brutal efficiency, drilled her in hand-to-hand combat. There were no rules, no holds barred. Anya endured bone-jarring strikes, learned to exploit weaknesses, and to fight dirty when necessary. She sparred with masked Network operatives, each encounter leaving her bruised and battered but also increasingly resilient. She learned to wield a variety of close-quarters weapons – a retractable wrist blade, a compact stun baton, even improvised tools fashioned from scraps of metal.

Mental discipline was just as crucial. Cipher, his fingers rarely leaving a data-slate, trained Anya's mind. He taught her the intricacies of Veridia's surveillance networks, how to identify blind spots, and how to move through the digital world unseen. She learned to memorize complex data streams, to decipher coded messages, and to recognize patterns in the flow of information. He pushed her memory to its limits, forcing her to recall intricate details under pressure.

Whisper oversaw her training, a constant, demanding presence. She taught Anya the art of observation, how to read body language, and how to blend seamlessly into any crowd. She drilled her in interrogation techniques, the subtle art of extracting information without resorting to overt violence – though that option was never entirely off the table. Whisper emphasized the importance of control, of masking her emotions, of becoming a chameleon in a city that thrived on surveillance.

There were days Anya felt like her body would break, her mind would shatter. The relentless pressure, the constant pain, the gnawing fear of failure – it all threatened to overwhelm her. She stumbled through drills, her movements clumsy, her focus fractured. Doubt whispered in the dark corners of her mind, questioning her ability to endure, to become the weapon the Network needed her to be.

But then, the memory of Elena's gentle smile and Misha's infectious laughter would resurface, a potent reminder of why she was enduring this torment. The burning desire for justice, for answers, for their safe return, fueled her through the pain. She learned to push past the exhaustion, to channel her anger into focus, to adapt and survive.

Slowly, almost imperceptibly at first, she began to master the skills. Her movements became more fluid, her strikes more precise. She could navigate the shadows with a growing confidence, her senses attuned to the subtle shifts in her environment. Her mind sharpened, able to process information quickly and efficiently.

One evening, after a particularly brutal combat session with Ronan, where she managed to disarm him for the first time, a rare flicker of approval crossed his scarred face. "You're learning, Petrova. You have the fire."

Even Whisper offered a rare nod of acknowledgement after Anya successfully infiltrated a simulated high-security zone without triggering any alarms. "You have potential. Don't waste it."

The rigorous training was forging Anya into something new, something harder, more dangerous. The street-smart survivor was evolving into a lethal operative, her grief and desperation being channeled into a focused, deadly skill set. The assassin within her was slowly awakening, honed by pain and driven by an unyielding love for her lost family. The first mission had been a bloody initiation. The next would demand even more.

Chapter 17

Weeks into her brutal training, Anya was pushed through a marksmanship drill. Ronan, his usual gruff demeanor amplified by the frustration of repeatedly having to reset targets, watched her struggle. The energy pistol felt foreign in her hand, the recoil unpredictable. Her shots consistently strayed wide of the designated zones.

"Focus, Petrova!" he barked, his voice echoing in the Network's makeshift firing range – a repurposed section of the abandoned subway tunnels. "Breathing. Sight alignment. Trigger control. It's not brute force!"

Anya gritted her teeth, frustration simmering. The fine motor skills required for accurate shooting seemed at odds with the raw, close-quarters combat she was slowly mastering. She took another shot, the energy bolt sizzling harmlessly into the wall.

Suddenly, as she adjusted her grip on the pistol, the faint blue light on the device hidden in a pouch on her belt pulsed rhythmically. At the exact same moment, a strange clarity washed over Anya. The jittery energy of the weapon seemed to stabilize in her hand. Her vision sharpened, the target rings becoming vividly distinct. Without conscious thought, her finger tightened on the trigger.

The energy bolt this time was a searing line of light that

punched through the center of the target with a satisfying thud. Ronan blinked in surprise.

"Beginner's luck," he grumbled, but a flicker of curiosity was in his eyes.

Anya tried again, focusing intently, but without the subtle pulse from the device, her shot went wide. She frowned, a dawning realization forming in her mind. Could there be a connection?

During the next round, she subtly pressed her hand against the pouch where the device rested. As the faint blue light pulsed, the same uncanny focus returned. Shot after shot, she drilled the center of the target, her movements fluid and precise, as if the weapon had become an extension of her own arm.

Ronan watched, his initial skepticism replaced by a growing astonishment. "What in the blazes... You've improved tenfold in a matter of seconds."

Later, during an infiltration exercise led by Lynx, Anya encountered a complex laser grid guarding a simulated data vault. Lynx had spent considerable time explaining the intricate patterns and the micro-second timing required to bypass it. Other trainees had struggled, triggering alarms with frustrating regularity.

As Anya approached the grid, the blue light on the device pulsed again. This time, instead of a feeling of focus, Anya experienced a strange visual overlay. Faint, almost imperceptible lines appeared in her vision, tracing the invisible pathways of the laser beams, revealing subtle fluctuations in their intensity and timing that were otherwise undetectable. It was as if the device was allowing her to see the unseen.

Moving with an intuitive grace, Anya weaved through the laser grid, her body flowing through the gaps with impossible precision. Lynx, observing from a control panel, stared in disbelief as Anya reached the vault without setting off a single alarm.

"That... that was remarkable, Anya," Lynx said, her voice laced with surprise. "Even seasoned operatives struggle with that configuration."

Anya herself was stunned. She hadn't consciously analyzed the laser patterns; she had simply... seen the way through.

The most significant demonstration of the device's unique properties came during a session with Cipher. He was attempting to crack a heavily encrypted corporate firewall, a simulation designed to test their digital intrusion skills. Anya, still a novice in the intricacies of hacking, watched him struggle against layers of complex code.

Frustrated, Cipher muttered, "This thing is a fortress. Standard brute-force methods are useless."

On a whim, Anya reached into her pouch and touched the device. As the blue light pulsed, she felt a strange resonance within her own neural interface. An almost instinctual understanding of the code on Cipher's screen flooded her mind. It wasn't that she suddenly understood the syntax, but rather, she could *feel* the pathways, the vulnerabilities, the subtle flaws in the digital architecture.

Without thinking, she reached for the keyboard and began to type, her fingers moving with a speed and precision that astonished even herself. Lines of code flowed from her fingertips, bypassing security protocols with an almost preternatural ease. The firewall, which had resisted Cipher's advanced techniques, crumbled before her.

Cipher stared at the screen, his jaw agape. "What... how did you do that? I've been working on this simulation for hours!"

Anya looked at her own hands, a sense of awe mixed with bewilderment. She didn't understand the code she had just manipulated, but the device... it had somehow given her the key.

Whisper, who had been observing the training sessions with increasing interest, approached Anya, her cybernetic eyes narrowed in contemplation. "That device you found... it's more than just a piece of old tech, isn't it?"

Anya nodded slowly, the implications of her unforeseen talents sinking in. "It... it seems to enhance my senses, my abilities. It showed me the gaps in the lasers, guided my aim... and it somehow allowed me to bypass that firewall."

Whisper's gaze was intense. "It's resonating with you, Anya. It's unlocking something within you. This changes things." The discovery of Anya's unique connection to the Spire device was no longer just a curiosity. It was a potential game-changer, a wild card that could tip the scales in their fight against the darkness of Veridia. And it raised a terrifying question: what else was this forgotten technology capable of?

Chapter 18

The revelation of Anya's connection to the Spire device sent a ripple of both excitement and concern through the Network. Her newfound abilities were undeniable assets, but Whisper cautioned restraint. "We don't understand its origins, Anya. Use it sparingly until we know more about its effects."

Weeks later, after extensive analysis by Cipher and the Network's tech specialists, they had a clearer, if still incomplete, understanding of the device.

"It's drawing power from you, Anya," Whisper explained, her voice grave. They were in the safehouse's training room, the walls lined with combat dummies and holographic target displays. "The device needs a considerable amount of energy to function at the levels you've been using it. And it's drawing that energy from your own bio-electric field."

Anya frowned. "Like... a battery?"

Cipher nodded, his fingers dancing across a data-slate displaying complex energy flow diagrams. "Essentially, yes. The Spire tech is incredibly advanced, far beyond anything we've seen in Veridia. It seems to interface directly with your nervous system, amplifying your senses and cognitive functions. But each time you use it, you're depleting your own energy reserves."

"And there are limits," Whisper added, her gaze intense. "The device is powerful, but it's not limitless. And neither are you. The headaches, the nosebleeds... they're warnings. Your body is telling you it can't sustain that level of energy output indefinitely."

Anya's stomach tightened. The price of her newfound abilities was higher than she had imagined. She had felt the drain, the exhaustion that followed each use of the device, but she had dismissed it as the cost of progress. Now, she understood the potential danger.

"What happens if I... push it too far?" she asked, her voice barely a whisper.

Whisper's expression was grim. "We don't know for sure. But the energy drain could become severe. Organ failure, neural damage... even death are possibilities. This tech is old and unstable."

The weight of that revelation settled heavily on Anya. The device was a lifeline, a key to finding her family and dismantling the network of corruption that had taken them. But it was also a potential death sentence.

"We've tried to find an external power source," Cipher said, his voice laced with frustration. "Something that could act as a buffer between you and the device. But the energy signature is unique, unlike anything we've encountered. It seems to be specifically calibrated to your bio-electric field."

"So I'm the only power source?" Anya asked, a sense of grim resignation washing over her.

Whisper placed a hand on Anya's shoulder, her touch surprisingly gentle. "Not necessarily. We're still exploring alternatives. But for now, you need to be extremely careful. Use the device only when absolutely necessary. We can't afford to lose you,

Anya. You're too valuable."

   The news was a heavy blow. Anya's reliance on the device had become almost instinctive, a crutch she had leaned on in moments of crisis. Now, she had to learn to manage its use, to balance the potential rewards against the very real risks to her own health. The path to finding her family had just become even more treacherous, not only from the external threats of Veridia's underbelly but from the very tool that had given her a fighting chance.

Chapter 19

Despite the crucial role the Spire device played in the Network's operations, a gnawing fear began to accompany Anya's every interaction with it. The headaches were becoming more intense, the nosebleeds more frequent and debilitating. The cold dread that washed over her after each use was a stark reminder of Whisper's grim warnings.

When Cipher needed her help to breach a secure Obsidian Hand communication hub, Anya hesitated. The digital fortress was a labyrinth of complex encryption, and Cipher admitted it would take him hours, time they didn't have. Her fingers hovered over the pouch containing the device, the familiar faint pulse a tempting whisper of power. But the memory of the last debilitating migraine, the metallic taste of blood in her mouth, held her back.

"Are you alright, Anya?" Cipher asked, noticing her hesitation.

"Just... thinking," she lied, her voice barely above a whisper. "Is there... another way?"

Cipher shook his head, his brow furrowed in concentration. "Not quickly. This level of encryption... it would take time we might not have."

Reluctantly, Anya reached for the device. As the blue light

pulsed, the digital walls crumbled before her, the pathways of data becoming intuitively clear. She guided Cipher with a speed and precision that even surprised him. The information they needed – encrypted communications detailing a planned transfer of "assets" – flowed onto the screen. But the price was immediate and sharp. A searing pain shot through her skull, and her vision swam with black spots. She had to lean heavily on the console to stay upright.

Whisper, observing Anya's distress, intervened. "That's enough, Anya. We have what we need. Rest." Her gaze was firm, a silent reprimand.

The assassinations also became a source of internal conflict, amplified by her fear of the device. When tasked with eliminating a key Obsidian Hand recruiter known for his network of informants, Anya found herself relying on the device to anticipate his movements in the crowded lower sectors. The heightened awareness allowed her to track him with unnerving accuracy, predicting his turns and interactions. But the closer she got, the more the physical toll mounted. By the time she finally confronted him, her head was pounding, and a trickle of blood had begun to stain her nostril. The act itself was swift and brutal, but the aftermath left her weak and trembling, the guilt compounded by the fear of what the device was doing to her.

During an infiltration mission to a suspected Obsidian Hand storage facility, Anya's fear almost compromised the operation. The facility was protected by an intricate network of laser grids and motion sensors. Remembering the sharp pain and disorientation that followed her previous use of the device, she hesitated, trying to rely solely on Lynx's instructions and her own training. She moved too slowly, triggering a proximity alarm that nearly alerted the guards. Lynx's sharp whisper of frustration echoed in her ear, a stark reminder that her fear could endanger them all. It was only in the face of immediate capture that Anya reluctantly activated the device, the familiar visual overlay allowing her to navigate the remaining defenses with a desperate, almost reckless speed. The subsequent nosebleed was one of the worst she had experienced, leaving her drained and shaken for hours.

With each mission, Anya's internal struggle intensified. The device was a powerful tool, essential for their fight, but its use was a constant reminder of her own vulnerability. She walked a tightrope between necessity and self-preservation, the fear of what the Spire technology was doing to her a heavy burden alongside the weight of her past actions and the desperate hope of finding her family. The shadows she now moved in held not only the threat of her enemies but also the chilling possibility of her own demise.

Chapter 20

The deeper Anya and Whisper delved into the Obsidian Hand's network, the more inconsistencies they uncovered regarding the organization's supposed motives for abducting individuals. While the evidence of organ trafficking and illicit tech trade was undeniable, some of the data Anya managed to extract, often at a significant personal cost, hinted at something more complex. Encrypted communications mentioned "Project Chimera" and "legacy assets," terms that didn't align with simple exploitation.

Whisper, initially focused on the broader implications of the Obsidian Hand's criminal enterprise, began to notice Anya's growing unease. "What is it, Anya? You've been... distant."

They were in the safehouse, poring over holographic schematics of a suspected Obsidian Hand research facility. Cipher was engrossed in his own analysis at a nearby console. Anya hesitated, her gaze fixed on a seemingly innocuous line of code that had triggered a flicker of unease within her, even without the aid of the device.

"Some of the data... it doesn't fit," Anya said slowly, keeping her voice low. "The missing persons files we cross-referenced with Thorne's ledger... some of them, the profiles... they weren't just random lower sector inhabitants. Some had... specialized skills. Technical expertise. Even... military backgrounds."

Whisper frowned, glancing towards the intently focused Cipher before leaning closer to Anya. "What are you suggesting?"

"It's just a feeling," Anya admitted, her voice barely above a whisper, "but it's like... they weren't just being taken for parts. Some of them felt... targeted. For something else."

Driven by Anya's intuition, Whisper initiated a deeper probe into the encrypted files, utilizing Cipher's advanced decryption algorithms when he wasn't directly looking. What they unearthed, in snatched moments when Cipher's attention was elsewhere, was fragmented but disturbing. Mentions of Anya's family name, Petrova, surfaced in heavily redacted documents linked to "Project Chimera." There were references to Elena's past – a surprisingly detailed record of her advanced engineering skills and a prior affiliation with a powerful, now defunct, research corporation. Misha's file, though less detailed, hinted at a unique genetic marker.

The revelation hit Anya like a physical blow. Her mother, a simple tech-mender in the Serpent's Coil, had a hidden past? Misha, her bright, innocent brother, possessed a unique genetic signature that someone deemed important? The carefully constructed image of her family's ordinary life shattered into a thousand pieces.

"Why didn't she ever tell me?" Anya whispered, her voice filled with confusion and a dawning sense of betrayal.

Whisper placed a hand on Anya's arm, her gaze intense but her voice kept low. "This changes everything, Anya. Your family... they might not have been random targets after all. This 'Project Chimera'... it could be the reason they were taken. And the Obsidian Hand... they might just be pawns in a larger game."

Just then, Whisper's wrist-mounted comm unit vibrated subtly. She glanced at it quickly, her cybernetic eyes scanning the brief message that flashed across its screen. Her expression tightened almost imperceptibly before she subtly deactivated it, ensuring Cipher remained unaware. The message was short, cryptic, and deeply unsettling: "Deception within. Trust no one. Legacy connection. Device key. Silence now."

Whisper turned back to Anya, her voice low and urgent, her gaze holding a new intensity. "Listen to me, Anya. This is crucial. For now, you need to keep what we've just discovered about your family, and... some other things I've just learned... completely to yourself. Don't mention it to Cipher, don't mention it to anyone else in the Network. Trust no one implicitly, not even me, entirely."

Her gaze hardened. "And most importantly... do not use the device. Not until we have a much clearer picture of what's happening. It makes you a target, and right now, we don't know who is truly on our side. Rely on your training, your instincts. We need to be more careful than ever."

Anya nodded slowly, the weight of Whisper's words settling heavily upon her. The path to finding her family had just become infinitely more treacherous, shrouded in layers of deception and hidden agendas. The only person she could truly rely on, it seemed, was herself. And the one tool that had given her power might now be her greatest vulnerability. The truth, she realized, was far more dangerous than the shadows, and even those who claimed to fight in the darkness might be playing a different game entirely.

Chapter 21

The rendezvous point, a dimly lit alcove behind a deactivated synth-ale dispensary in the Serpent's Coil, felt exposed and vulnerable. Anya, her senses on high alert, scanned the passing faces, her wariness a constant companion. Whisper's instructions had been stark: *Deliver Griffin to the safehouse in the Foundry District. No one else needs to know the route. Trust your instincts.* The secrecy surrounding this particular delivery, even within the Network, amplified Anya's inherent suspicion.

Griffin, a young man with nervous energy radiating off him in waves, clutched a tightly sealed data-drive. His eyes darted around the alleyway, reflecting the flickering neon signs like trapped insects. Jax, the contact who had facilitated the initial meeting, had vanished with his credits, leaving Anya with a palpable sense of unease.

The journey across Veridia was a tightrope walk. Anya chose a circuitous route, weaving through crowded transport hubs, deserted service tunnels, and across the precarious rooftops of the mid-levels. With each change of scenery, her vigilance remained unwavering. She couldn't shake the feeling of being watched, of unseen eyes tracking their progress. Was it the Obsidian Hand, anticipating their move? Or was there a leak within the Network itself, given the unusual secrecy surrounding this delivery?

As they navigated the bustling Foundry District, a sector known for its heavy industry and rough inhabitants, a sudden commotion erupted nearby. A group of hulking figures, their faces obscured by crude cybernetic masks, shoved their way through the crowd, their attention fixed on Griffin. Anya's training kicked in instantly. These weren't random thugs; their focused aggression suggested a targeted interception.

"Run!" Anya hissed at Griffin, shoving him towards a narrow alleyway. A brief but brutal skirmish ensued. Anya moved with a lethal efficiency, her stun baton cracking against bone and metal. The attackers were relentless, their movements suggesting a familiarity with Network tactics. This realization sent a cold shiver down Anya's spine. How could they have known their location, their objective?

Escaping the ambush, Anya altered their route again, plunging them deeper into the Foundry's grimy underbelly. The pursuit, though not sustained, left a lingering sense of vulnerability. Every shadow seemed to conceal a potential enemy, every passing vehicle a possible threat. Anya's hand remained close to her concealed wrist blade, her trust in anyone beyond herself and Whisper eroding with each passing moment.

Finally, they reached the designated safehouse, a nondescript fabrication workshop tucked away in a labyrinthine industrial complex. Silas greeted them at the heavily fortified entrance, his usual stoic demeanor betraying a flicker of concern. As Griffin was secured inside, Silas's gaze met Anya's, a silent acknowledgment of the perilous journey.

Later, in the relative quiet of the safehouse, Anya's unease remained palpable. The ambush in the Foundry District had been too precise, too targeted. She sought out Whisper, her voice low and troubled. "That ambush... it wasn't random. They knew we were coming for Griffin."

Whisper's cybernetic eyes held a steady gaze. "The Obsidian Hand has resources, Anya. Griffin is valuable. An interception attempt was a possibility we anticipated." But there was a subtle coolness in her tone, a carefully guarded expression that did little to reassure Anya. The secrecy surrounding Griffin's delivery, the coordinated attack – it all pointed towards a potential breach, a leak that only a select few within the Network would have knowledge of. And in the murky world of shadows and secrets, trust was a luxury Anya could no longer afford. The perilous delivery had been completed, but it had left a bitter taste of suspicion and a gnawing certainty that the true danger lay not just outside the Network, but perhaps within its very ranks.

Chapter 22

The escort mission had taken a sharp turn when they were ambushed in the Foundry District. As Anya and Griffin scrambled through the grimy back alleys, pursued by the relentless, masked figures, Griffin stumbled, his ankle twisting on a loose piece of synth-crete. A sharp cry of pain escaped his lips, and he collapsed against a rusted transport container.

Anya whirled around, her stun baton charged. The masked pursuers were gaining on them, their heavy boots pounding on the grimy pavement. Griffin was slowing them down, making them both vulnerable.

"I can't... I can't run," Griffin gasped, his face contorted in pain. He clutched his data-drive tightly. "Just... take the drive. Get it to Silas."

Anya's mind raced. Whisper's instructions were clear: deliver Griffin. But the pursuers were closing in, their intent undoubtedly lethal. Leaving Griffin meant ensuring the data-drive reached the Network, potentially uncovering vital information about Project Chimera and, by extension, her family. But abandoning him felt like a betrayal, a cold echo of the indifference the Enforcers had shown her own plight.

"We go together," Anya said, her voice firm, though a knot of doubt tightened in her stomach.

But Griffin shook his head vehemently. "No. They want the information. If you get it to Silas... it won't be for nothing. Don't let them get it." He looked at her with desperate urgency. "Please. You have to."

The masked figures rounded the corner, their weapons – crude energy pistols – raised. Anya had mere seconds to decide. Her loyalty to the Network, to the mission, screamed to protect the data-drive at all costs. But the ingrained sense of responsibility, the refusal to leave someone behind to the wolves, warred fiercely within her.

A brutal calculation flashed through her mind. She could try to defend Griffin, but their chances against multiple armed attackers, with Griffin injured, were slim. Both the data-drive and Griffin could be lost. Leaving him, however agonizing, offered a chance – a chance for the information to reach the Network, a chance to unravel the truth.

With a wrenching internal struggle, Anya made her choice. "I'm sorry," she choked out, her eyes locking with Griffin's for a fleeting moment, a silent promise of retribution. She grabbed the data-drive from his outstretched hand and turned, sprinting into the maze of alleyways, the sounds of Griffin's pained cries and the crackle of energy weapons echoing behind her.

Guilt gnawed at her with every step. The ruthlessness her training had instilled, the cold calculus of mission priority over individual life, had just been brutally tested. She had chosen the mission, chosen the data-drive, chosen to leave a vulnerable man to face his attackers alone.

Reaching the relative safety of the Foundry's deeper shadows, Anya's breath came in ragged gasps. The data-drive felt heavy in her hand, a tangible weight of her decision. She had secured the package, fulfilled her immediate objective. But the cost... the cost was Griffin's life, a life she might have been able to save if she had made a different choice.

Delivering the data-drive to a somber Silas in the safehouse felt hollow. The information it contained – detailed schematics of an OmniCorp facility involved in genetic research – was significant, potentially a key to understanding Project Chimera. But the victory felt tainted, stained by the image of Griffin's desperate face.

Later, Whisper found Anya alone in a quiet corner of the safehouse, her face pale and drawn. "You delivered the package, Anya. Silas says the information is valuable."

Anya looked up, her eyes filled with a raw pain that went beyond physical exhaustion. "I left him, Whisper. I left Griffin. They... they were going to kill him."

Whisper's expression was unreadable. "You followed protocol, Anya. The mission objective was paramount. Griffin understood the risks."

"But was it right?" Anya's voice was barely a whisper. "To just... leave him?"

Whisper was silent for a long moment. "Survival in this world often demands difficult choices, Anya. Choices that weigh heavily on the soul. The Network operates in the shadows to make the greater good possible, even if it means sacrificing the few."

But Anya wasn't sure she believed it anymore. The cold logic of the mission felt inadequate against the searing guilt in her heart. She had made a choice, a choice driven by the ruthlessness her training had demanded. But the consequences of that choice would forever mark her, a stark reminder of the moral crossroads she had faced and the path she had taken. The data-drive held the promise of truth, but it was stained with the blood of her conscience.

Chapter 23

Sleep offered no escape for Anya. Griffin's face, contorted in pain and resignation, haunted her dreams. The echo of energy fire and his choked plea for her to take the data-drive replayed endlessly in her mind. The Network's cold justification – the greater good – felt like a hollow excuse for her own agonizing decision.

The next morning, Anya sought out Whisper, her eyes red-rimmed and her voice raw with desperation. "Whisper, I need to go back."

Whisper, who was reviewing the data extracted from Griffin's drive, looked up, her expression guarded. "Back where, Anya?"

"To the Foundry District," Anya pleaded. "To Griffin. Maybe... maybe he's still alive. Maybe I can help him."

Whisper's cybernetic eyes scanned Anya's face, assessing the raw emotion etched there. "Anya, be realistic. You said they were armed. The longer you wait, the less likely his survival becomes. And returning puts you, and the data he risked his life for, in jeopardy."

"But I left him!" Anya's voice cracked. "I just... ran. The Network's way... it felt so cold. I can't just leave him to die if there's even a chance..."

Whisper sighed, a rare display of something akin to weariness.

"Anya, you followed the mission parameters. You secured the intel. That was paramount."

"But at what cost?" Anya countered, her voice rising in anguish. "He helped us. He trusted us. And I just... abandoned him."

"The Obsidian Hand doesn't offer second chances," Whisper said, her tone firm. "Returning is foolish. It's driven by emotion, not logic. It could compromise everything we've gained."

"Logic?" Anya scoffed, a bitter laugh escaping her lips. "Is it logical to just leave someone to die? Is that the kind of person the Network wants me to be?"

The question hung heavy in the air. Whisper remained silent for a long moment, her gaze unwavering. Finally, she spoke, her voice softer than before, but still resolute. "Anya, I understand your feelings. But we operate in a world where difficult choices are often the only choices. Griffin knew the risks. You did what you had to do."

"But I need to know," Anya insisted, tears welling in her eyes. "I need to know if I could have done something more. If I just left him to die for nothing."

Whisper studied Anya's distraught face. A flicker of something – perhaps understanding, perhaps a reluctant empathy – crossed her features. "Going back is dangerous, Anya. I won't order you to do it. But if you are determined... you will go alone. The Network cannot risk resources on a rescue mission with such low probability of success."

Anya met Whisper's gaze, a fragile spark of hope igniting within her despite the stark warning. "I understand. Just... can you help me get back there? Discreetly? Without alerting anyone?"

Whisper hesitated, then nodded slowly. "I can provide you

with transport and some basic recon data of the area. But Anya... be careful. Don't let your emotions cloud your judgment. And if it's a trap... you need to be ready to walk away."

The journey back to the Foundry District felt like a descent into her own guilt. The rain-slicked alleys where she had left Griffin seemed to echo with his pain. The area was deserted now, the earlier commotion vanished as if it had never happened.

Anya moved cautiously, her senses on high alert. She found the spot where Griffin had fallen, a dark stain on the synth-crete the only evidence of the struggle. She searched the surrounding alleys, her heart pounding with a desperate hope that he might have somehow survived, might have crawled away.

But there was no sign of him. Only the cold, uncaring indifference of the city. The silence was deafening, broken only by the distant hum of Veridia's relentless machinery.

As the grim reality sank in, a wave of despair washed over Anya. She had come back, driven by a sliver of hope, but found only emptiness. Whether Griffin was dead or captured, her return had yielded nothing but the crushing weight of her regret. The Network's cold logic, she realized with a bitter pang, was often the brutal truth of their existence. And Anya was now forced to confront the kind of person that truth was shaping her into. The ghost of Griffin would follow her, a constant reminder of the moral crossroads and the path she had chosen.

Chapter 24

Haunted by Griffin's fate and the Network's stark pragmatism, Anya sought a mission that offered a semblance of solitude and a chance to process her fractured conscience. Under the guise of scouting a potential Obsidian Hand data relay point in the less-trafficked periphery of the mid-levels, she requested a solo assignment. Whisper, observing Anya's withdrawn demeanor, reluctantly agreed, providing minimal intel and a silent transport drone.

The designated facility was a dilapidated comms relay station, its antennae reaching like skeletal fingers towards the smog-choked sky. Anya moved through the echoing, dust-filled chambers, her senses sharp despite the turmoil within. She found no active data streams, just outdated equipment and the ghosts of forgotten transmissions. As she prepared to report her findings, a faint, unusual energy signature drew her towards a sealed-off sub-level.

Bypassing the corroded access panel, Anya descended into a cramped, dimly lit workshop. At its center, connected to a humming diagnostic unit, was a piece of technology that sparked an immediate, unsettling recognition. It was a Spire interface, smaller and more portable than the analysis unit she had briefly glimpsed in the pickle-jar facility (a memory that now felt strangely disconnected from reality), but unmistakably of the same origin. Its faint blue light pulsed with a familiar, almost sentient rhythm.

As Anya cautiously approached, she noticed a series of data logs scrolling across the diagnostic unit's screen. Her breath hitched as she began to decipher them. The logs detailed energy fluctuations and bio-signature readings associated with Spire technology. One entry, timestamped shortly before the ambush, contained a detailed analysis of a "fluctuating energy spike" detected near Griffin's last known coordinates during transport.

But it wasn't correlated with Griffin.

As Anya scrolled further down, her blood ran cold. The analysis focused not on Griffin's bio-signature, but on a separate, distinct energy resonance, one that matched the unique signature of the Spire device. *Her* device. The logs tracked its activation, its subtle pulses as she navigated the Foundry's alleys, its heightened output as she fought off the initial attackers.

A wave of nausea and a chilling realization washed over Anya. The ambush wasn't about Griffin. It was about *her*. The Obsidian Hand hadn't been after the data-drive; they had been after the Spire device, and by extension, her. Griffin had been collateral damage, a casualty in a hunt for her and the technology she carried.

The weight of this truth crashed down on Anya with crushing force. She had blamed the Network's cold pragmatism, her own ruthless training, for Griffin's death. But the responsibility was hers. Her connection to the device, her reliance on its power, had made them a target. She had led those killers to Griffin, sealed his fate with her own actions.

The seemingly abandoned comms relay station suddenly felt like a tomb, filled with the ghosts of her guilt and the chilling echo of her culpability. The mission to clear her head had instead revealed a horrifying truth: she was the hunted, and her pursuit of justice had come at a devastating, personal cost. The shadows she moved in were not just filled with enemies, but with the consequences of her own choices.

Chapter 25

As Anya remained hidden in the shadowed workshop, a faint mechanical whir reached her ears, followed by the soft hiss of a door panel sliding open. She instantly froze, melting deeper into the gloom behind a towering stack of defunct signal boosters. Low voices drifted into the room, laced with an urgency that sent a shiver down her spine.

"...the energy readings are stable. She's close." It was Silas's voice, stripped of its usual stoic neutrality, replaced by a cold, clinical tone Anya had never heard before.

"Excellent," Cipher's voice replied, its familiar cadence now carrying a chilling undercurrent of command. "The device's potential for subject enhancement is significant. If we can just sever its connection to her..."

Anya's breath hitched. Subject? Enhancement? They weren't just after the device; they were after her, her unique bond with the Spire technology.

Silas and Cipher stepped fully into the workshop, followed by several figures clad in sterile lab coats, their faces illuminated by the soft glow of their data-pads. They carried an array of unfamiliar equipment, humming softly with contained energy.

"The resonance is strongest in this sector," one of the lab-coated individuals murmured, their gaze sweeping across the cluttered space. "She can't be far."

Silas's eyes scanned the room, sharp and assessing. They lingered for a disconcerting moment on the very shadows where Anya was concealed, a flicker of something – perhaps awareness, perhaps a hunter sensing its prey – crossing his face before it settled back into a mask of cold determination.

"Locate her," Silas commanded, his voice low and precise. "Retrieve the device. And if she resists... ensure she presents no further complications."

Anya's heart pounded against her ribs. The pieces of the puzzle, though not fully assembled, sent a jolt of fear through her. Silas's intense focus on the device, Cipher's chilling words about "enhancement" – it all pointed to a deeper agenda, one that made her connection to the Spire technology far more significant, and far more dangerous, than she had ever imagined. The Network, her only hope, now felt like a hunting ground. The only certainty in this growing web of unease was the cryptic warning Whisper had given her: *Trust no one.* Anya knew then that her survival depended on her own instincts and the desperate need to understand the true nature of the forces closing in around her.

Chapter 26

The air in the workshop crackled with tension. Anya, pressed against the cold metal of a defunct signal booster, could feel the vibrations of the scanning equipment as the lab-coated figures methodically swept the room. Silas's cold command echoed in her ears: *Retrieve the device. Ensure she presents no further complications.* The words were a death knell.

Her own data-pad, a standard Network issue, felt like a tracking beacon in her pocket. Cipher, with his mastery of their systems, could pinpoint her location with ease. She had to sever that connection, become a ghost in their digital machine.

Moving with a slow, deliberate grace honed by weeks of training, Anya edged along the wall, her senses straining for any sound that might betray her. The team was focused on their scanners, their movements methodical but predictable. She needed an opening, a moment of distraction.

Her gaze fell upon a junction box mounted on the wall, its wires exposed and sparking intermittently. It was a long shot, but it was the only option that presented itself. If she could create a localized power surge, it might disrupt their equipment, give her the precious seconds she needed.

Timing her movements with the rhythmic sweep of a scanner, Anya darted towards the junction box. Her fingers, nimble and quick, worked at the loose panel, pulling it open just enough to access the chaotic tangle of wires within. She needed to overload a specific circuit, something that would cause a temporary power fluctuation without triggering a full system shutdown that would immediately alert them.

Remembering a basic electrical principle Cipher had briefly touched upon during a rudimentary tech-evasion lesson, Anya identified two wires of contrasting color. Taking a deep breath, she risked a quick, controlled touch, bridging the gap between them with a small, discarded piece of metal she found amongst the debris.

A sharp crackle of energy erupted from the junction box, accompanied by a shower of sparks. The lights in the workshop flickered violently, and the humming of the scanning equipment stuttered and died. A collective murmur of confusion rippled through the search team.

"What was that?" Silas's voice cut through the momentary chaos, laced with annoyance.

"Power surge, sir," one of the lab technicians stammered, fiddling with his unresponsive scanner. "My readings are gone."

This was Anya's chance. Using the confusion as cover, she moved swiftly and silently towards the exit. Her own data-pad was still active, a digital leash around her neck. She needed to disable it, and she needed to do it quickly and without being seen.

Slipping into the darkened corridor, Anya found a small maintenance alcove. Inside, amongst cleaning supplies and discarded tools, was a heavy-duty utility knife. It wasn't elegant, but it would serve its purpose.

Her fingers worked quickly, accessing the data-pad's internal casing. She located the power cell and, with a decisive movement, plunged the utility knife into it. A small hiss of escaping energy and the faint smell of burnt circuitry filled the air. The data-pad went dark, its tracking capabilities silenced.

She was no longer a blip on their digital radar. She was a ghost, moving through their hunting grounds unseen. The surge had bought her precious time, and the disabled data-pad had severed their connection. Now, her only goal was to escape the facility and find Whisper, the only beacon of trust in a world that had suddenly turned treacherous. The path ahead was fraught with danger, but for the first time since realizing the potential betrayal, Anya felt a sliver of control. She was no longer the hunted; she was the unseen, and she would use the shadows to her advantage.

Chapter 27

Anya moved through the darkened corridors of the comms relay facility like a phantom, the silence amplifying the frantic beat of her heart. The revelation of Silas and Cipher's treachery had ripped away the last vestiges of her trust in the Network. Their talk of "subject enhancement" and coldly efficient neutralization sent a chill deeper than any Veridian night. She had to escape, had to reach Whisper, the only potential ally in this viper's nest.

As she navigated a maze of ventilation shafts, a familiar voice, laced with urgency, echoed through the metal conduits. "Anya? Anya, can you hear me?" It was Whisper, her tone a mixture of concern and something else... fear?

Anya froze, her hand instinctively reaching for a length of discarded cable she had fashioned into a makeshift weapon. Whisper. The only one she thought she could trust. But the tendrils of suspicion had spread, poisoning her every instinct. Could Whisper be part of it too? Had the warning to trust no one been a carefully orchestrated manipulation?

"Anya, please respond!" Whisper's voice was closer now, tinged with desperation. "Silas and Cipher... they raised an alarm. They know you're there. I can help you get out."

Doubt gnawed at Anya. Why was Whisper helping her? Was

CHAPTER 27

this a genuine offer of aid, or a calculated move to lure her into a trap? The image of Silas's cold eyes and Cipher's chilling command flashed in her mind. She couldn't risk it.

Without responding, Anya shifted direction, crawling silently through a branching ventilation shaft, putting distance between herself and Whisper's voice.

"Anya, wait!" Whisper's plea echoed behind her, laced with a growing panic. "You don't understand! What they're doing... it's far worse than you can imagine!"

Anya hesitated for a fraction of a second, the desperation in Whisper's voice tugging at her resolve. But the ingrained paranoia, the raw sting of potential betrayal, held her captive. She couldn't risk trusting anyone, not yet. Not until she understood the full scope of the deception.

Emerging from a maintenance hatch into a deserted loading bay, Anya spotted a dilapidated transport drone, its power core flickering erratically. It was a long shot, but it was her only way out.

"Anya, please! They're not just after the device!" Whisper's voice was closer now, she must have tracked Anya's movements through the facility's internal sensors. "They're... they're making something, Anya. With the missing people. It's not about donors, not just parts. It's... something else. Something terrible."

The words hung in the air, heavy with an unspoken horror. Making something? With the missing people? Not donors? A cold dread seeped into Anya's bones, eclipsing even her fear of betrayal. What could be so sinister that it made Whisper sound so truly terrified?

"Anya, please! They took your mother... Silas was involved from the start!" Whisper's voice was right behind her now, her hand reaching out. "They needed someone with her neural architecture for... for what they're building!"

The confirmation of Silas's betrayal, the chilling implication of her mother's unique role in whatever horrific project they were undertaking, slammed into Anya with brutal force. Her heart twisted with a raw mixture of anguish and a desperate need to understand.

Spotting a loose panel on the transport drone, Anya ripped it open, exposing a tangle of wires. Years of scraping by in the Serpent's Coil had taught her a thing or two about jury-rigging technology. Ignoring Whisper's frantic pleas, Anya began to splice wires, her movements fueled by adrenaline and a desperate need to escape.

"Anya, no! You don't understand the danger you're in! What they're making... it will change everything!" Whisper's voice was right behind her now, her hand reaching out.

Anya flinched away, her eyes filled with a raw mixture of fear and grief. With a final, desperate connection, the transport drone's engine sputtered to life. Ignoring Whisper's outstretched hand and her desperate cries, Anya clambered into the cockpit, the ancient machinery groaning beneath her.

With a lurch and a shower of sparks, the transport drone lifted off the ground, leaving Whisper standing alone in the deserted loading bay, her anguished pleas fading into the roar of the struggling engine. Anya looked back for a fleeting moment, seeing the raw desperation on Whisper's face, a desperation that almost broke through her wall of distrust. But the image of Silas's cold eyes and Cipher's chilling words propelled her forward, away from the only potential ally she had left, soaring into the uncertain night sky, a fugitive adrift in a city teeming with unseen enemies, the horrifying words "they're making

CHAPTER 27

something" echoing in her mind.

Chapter 28

The dilapidated transport drone rattled through the underbelly of Veridia, a metal coffin against the neon-drenched cityscape. Anya gripped the controls, her knuckles white, her mind a whirlwind of conflicting emotions and fractured trust. The roar of the failing engine was a constant, deafening reminder of her isolation.

Whisper's desperate words echoed in her head: *"They're making something... it's not about donors... something terrible... Silas was involved from the start... they needed someone with her neural architecture... for what they're building!"*

The Network, once a beacon of hope, now felt like a mirage, dissolving into the harsh reality of betrayal. Silas, the stoic figure of authority, now wore the face of a serpent. Cipher, the master of information, was a puppeteer pulling strings she couldn't see. Lynx, Ronan, the others – their faces were now masks, their loyalties suspect. The very foundation of her understanding had crumbled.

Anya found a precarious landing spot on a deserted rooftop in a forgotten sector, the silence here a stark contrast to the drone's mechanical caterwauling. Cutting the power, she was plunged into near darkness, the distant glow of Veridia's towers casting long, distorted shadows.

CHAPTER 28

Alone. Truly alone for the first time since Whisper had pulled her from the Enforcer raid. The weight of that isolation pressed down on her, heavier than any physical burden. She had severed her connection to the only person who had offered consistent help, driven by a distrust that now felt both necessary and terrifyingly lonely.

Doubt gnawed at her. What if Whisper had been telling the truth? The desperation in her voice had sounded genuine. The revelation about her mother's unique neural architecture... it resonated with the fragmented memories of Elena's brilliance, her almost intuitive understanding of complex technology. What if Anya, with her own connection to the Spire device, was somehow linked to this horrific "making something"?

But the ingrained caution, the hard-won survival instincts of the Serpent's Coil, wouldn't let her fully surrender to that possibility. The betrayal by Silas and Cipher felt too real, too calculated. To trust again so quickly felt like a fool's errand, a step back into the jaws of the beast.

She pulled the Spire device from her pouch, its faint blue pulse a constant companion. It had granted her power, insight, a connection to something ancient and unknown. But it had also made her a target, a pawn in a game far larger and more sinister than she could have imagined. Was this device the key to understanding what they were "making"? Was it the reason her mother was taken?

Every memory of her time with the Network was now tainted with suspicion. Had their training been genuine, or a way to mold her, to control her connection to the device? Had their missions served a larger, hidden agenda? The faces of her former allies now seemed to hold veiled intentions, their words carrying unspoken meanings.

Anya felt adrift, a small boat tossed on a stormy sea of deceit. The price of truth in Veridia seemed to be the complete dismantling of everything she thought she knew. The lines between justice and vengeance had blurred, and now, the lines between friend and enemy were indistinguishable. Her only compass was a desperate need for answers, a burning desire to understand what they had done to her family, and a gnawing fear of the terrifying "something" they were creating in the shadows. And in this isolation, questioning everything, Anya knew one thing for certain: she was on her own.

Chapter 29

The cold reality of her isolation settled deep within Anya, a hard knot of resolve tightening in her chest. The Network was no longer a sanctuary; it was a cage, its promises of justice revealed as elaborate lies. Silas's betrayal, Cipher's chilling ambition, Whisper's desperate but ultimately untrusted pleas – they painted a clear picture. Anya was a pawn in a game she didn't understand, and the players on both sides were ruthless.

The dilapidated transport drone became her escape vessel, a sputtering lifeline carrying her away from the crumbling edifice of her former allegiance. Landing on the rain-slicked rooftop of a derelict data storage facility in the Outer Rings, Anya knew she couldn't stay still. The Network's surveillance was pervasive; they would be tracking her. And the organization that had snatched her family, now revealed to be intertwined with Silas and Cipher's sinister "making something," would be hunting her too, especially if her unique connection to the Spire device was crucial to their plans.

Anya moved with a newfound urgency, a ghost slipping through the city's underbelly. The skills the Network had drilled into her were now her only defense, repurposed for survival against her former allies. She avoided established routes, sticking to the forgotten pathways and the digital blind spots she had learned to identify. The Spire device, nestled in her pocket, was a constant reminder of her hunted status, its faint blue pulse a beacon to those who sought to control it.

Her first priority was to disappear, to become untraceable. She needed to shed her Network identity, erase her digital footprint. This meant diving deep into the chaotic anonymity of Veridia's black markets and the encrypted corners of the net. Using her limited credits and bartering for favors with contacts she had made during her brief time in the shadows, Anya began to dismantle her digital self. She cycled through burner comms, routed her meager funds through untraceable crypto-wallets, and scrubbed her presence from Network databases using the rudimentary hacking skills Cipher had reluctantly taught her.

The process was slow and fraught with risk. Every connection, every transaction, was a potential point of exposure. The Network's digital reach was vast, and she could feel their electronic tendrils probing the darkness, searching for her. The chilling awareness that Silas and Cipher were actively hunting her, their resources far exceeding her own, fueled her relentless efforts.

As she navigated the treacherous landscape of the digital underground, Anya couldn't shake the memory of Whisper's desperate words. *"They're making something... it's not about donors... something terrible... Silas was involved from the start... they needed someone with her neural architecture... for what they're building!"* The horrifying implications of that statement spurred her on. She wasn't just running for her own survival; she was running to uncover the truth about her mother, about the sinister project that had torn her family apart.

Anya found temporary refuge in a squalid, forgotten corner of the Undercity, a place where even the Enforcers rarely dared to tread. Huddled in the darkness, she finally allowed herself a moment of respite. The city's grimy air filled her lungs, a stark contrast to the sterile environment of the safehouse. She was alone, hunted, stripped of her allegiances. But beneath the fear and the exhaustion, a new resolve began to solidify. She would not be a pawn. She would not be silenced. She would uncover their lies, even if it meant tearing down the entire Network and facing the monstrous truth of what they were "making." Anya Petrova, once a reluctant recruit, was now truly rogue, a ghost in the system, and the hunt had just begun.

Chapter 30

Anya's flight from the Network had thrown her into a far more perilous landscape. She was no longer just evading the organization that had abducted her family; now, the Network itself was a relentless hunter, their resources and knowledge of her capabilities a significant threat. And the Enforcers, alerted to her rogue status and the chaos she had left behind, were another relentless force closing in. She was caught between two hells, each determined to capture or eliminate her.

Survival became a minute-to-minute calculation. Anya relied on the fragmented knowledge gleaned from her Network training, blending into the city's teeming underbelly, utilizing its forgotten pathways and exploiting the jurisdictional boundaries between different Enforcer sectors. Sleep was a luxury she could rarely afford, replaced by a constant state of vigilance. Every shadow held a potential threat, every passing vehicle could be carrying her pursuers.

The Spire device, once a source of power and insight, was now a liability. Its unique energy signature could be tracked, making her a walking beacon. Anya kept it shielded as best she could, wrapping it in layers of scavenged conductive material, hoping to dampen its emissions. But the constant fear of detection weighed heavily on her.

CHAPTER 30

Her focus remained laser-sharp: uncover the truth behind Project Chimera and the real players pulling the strings. The Network's lies had made it clear they were not the ultimate authority. Silas and Cipher were taking orders from someone else, someone with the resources and influence to manipulate a powerful organization like the Network.

Anya's investigation began with the fragmented data she had managed to access before her escape. The OmniCorp connection was a key thread. She sought out the dark corners of the net, the encrypted forums and black market data brokers, searching for any whisper, any rumor related to OmniCorp and "Project Chimera." The information was heavily guarded, often encrypted behind layers of sophisticated security.

She used the rudimentary hacking skills Cipher had taught her, augmented by the intuitive nudges from the Spire device (used sparingly, mindful of its tracking potential), to probe the edges of OmniCorp's digital fortress. What she found was deeply disturbing: heavily redacted research logs, references to neural manipulation, and cryptic mentions of "integrated assets." The language was clinical, dehumanizing, painting a picture of a project far more sinister than simple organ harvesting.

As Anya dug deeper, she encountered resistance. Her attempts to access certain files triggered alarms, and she could feel the digital counter-attacks, the probing algorithms of sophisticated security systems trying to pinpoint her location. The Network's digital hounds were on her trail.

The Enforcers were a more physical threat. Wanted posters bearing her face began to appear in the lower sectors. Patrols were intensified in areas she frequented. She had to constantly change her appearance, utilizing disguises and exploiting the anonymity of the city's vast population. Close calls became a regular occurrence, forcing her to rely on her agility and the art of blending into the urban landscape.

Caught between these two relentless forces, Anya knew she couldn't remain a ghost forever. She needed allies, information, a way to strike back. The truth about Project Chimera, and the fate of her mother, lay hidden behind layers of corporate secrecy and Network deception. And Anya, alone and hunted, was determined to unearth it, even if it cost her everything. The neon shadows of Veridia had become her battleground, and the price of truth was a fight for survival against two powerful enemies.

Chapter 31

Anya found temporary refuge in a derelict freight elevator shaft, clinging to rusted rungs high above the grimy factory floor. The silence was a welcome reprieve from the constant paranoia that gnawed at her. But the reprieve was short-lived. A faint ping from a scavenged scanner she had repurposed as a rudimentary threat detector alerted her to approaching figures. Network operatives.

They moved with a coordinated precision that spoke of their training, their hushed comms barely audible in the cavernous space. Anya knew they were hunting her, their movements suggesting they were tracking her residual digital signature or perhaps even anticipating her escape routes.

Adrenaline surged through her veins. This was it. Her first direct confrontation with the Network since going rogue. Without the Spire device amplifying her senses and reflexes, she would have to rely solely on the skills they had taught her, skills now turned against their own.

As the operatives rappelled down the shaft, their forms silhouetted against the faint light filtering from below, Anya prepared for a fight. She moved silently, positioning herself for an ambush. The first operative reached her level, his weapon – a compact energy pistol – raised. Anya reacted instantly, using the rusted rungs for leverage, launching herself in a swift, brutal takedown. The operative crashed against the metal wall, stunned.

But the others were quick. Energy bolts sizzled past her head, forcing her to take cover behind a thick support beam. She moved with agility, dodging and weaving, utilizing the confined space to her advantage. Her hand-to-hand combat skills, honed through relentless training, were sharp and effective. She disarmed another operative with a swift series of strikes, using their own momentum against them.

Yet, a stark realization began to dawn. Without the almost precognitive awareness the Spire device granted her, she was slower, less precise. The subtle tells in her opponents' movements, the split-second anticipations that had become almost second nature, were now harder to discern. She was good, better than most, but she wasn't the enhanced operative she had become with the device. She was Anya Petrova, street kid turned Network recruit, fighting on instinct and adrenaline.

One of the operatives, more experienced than the others, managed to land a glancing blow with an energy blast. Pain seared through her arm, momentarily numbing her fingers. The realization hit her with the force of a physical blow: she couldn't win this fight. Not without the device. Not against a coordinated team.

Her objective wasn't to stand and fight; it was to survive, to uncover the truth. Engaging them further would only lead to capture or worse. With a burst of speed, she used a smoke pellet she had scavenged, the acrid fumes filling the confined space, obscuring their vision.

"She's getting away!" she heard Silas's voice, amplified through their comms, cutting through the chaos. "Seal the exits!"

But Anya was already moving. Utilizing a narrow maintenance tunnel she had spotted earlier, she scrambled away, the sounds of the frustrated operatives echoing behind her. The chase was on.

Emerging into the labyrinthine corridors of the abandoned factory, Anya didn't hesitate. She ran. She ran with the desperation of a cornered animal, her injured arm throbbing, her lungs burning. The Network was hunting her with a renewed ferocity, and the chilling awareness of what they were "making" fueled her flight. She had to survive. She had to find a way to expose their lies and uncover the truth, even if it meant leaving behind the ghost of the enhanced operative she had briefly become. Anya Petrova, stripped of her power, was now a fugitive, her only advantage her knowledge of the shadows and an unyielding will to survive.

Chapter 32

The city had turned against Anya. Her face, stark and defiant, stared down from countless holographic wanted signs plastered across every available surface – transit hubs, market stalls, even the grimy walls of the Undercity. The Network's reach was insidious, their propaganda painting her as a dangerous rogue, a traitor who had turned against their noble cause. The Enforcers, undoubtedly receiving their own heavily biased briefings, were conducting city-wide sweeps, their armored vehicles a constant, ominous presence.

Anya was a painted target, every citizen a potential informant eager for the hefty bounty on her head. The anonymity of the crowds, once her greatest asset, now felt like a suffocating trap. Every glance held suspicion, every hushed conversation felt like it was about her. Simple acts of survival – acquiring food, finding temporary shelter – became high-stakes gambles.

The shadows, once her sanctuary, offered little respite. Network operatives, their faces grim and determined, patrolled the underlevels, their enhanced senses and tracking technology making her every footstep a risk. The Enforcers, with their brute force and advanced surveillance systems, blanketed the main thoroughfares. Anya was squeezed between two relentless forces, the walls of her hiding places closing in.

CHAPTER 32

Desperation gnawed at her. She was running out of options, running out of places to disappear. The city, her familiar hunting ground, had become a cage. The chilling realization settled upon her: she couldn't do this alone. She lacked the resources, the information, the sheer manpower to fight both the Network and the Enforcers while simultaneously uncovering the truth about Project Chimera.

One name echoed in the desolate corners of her mind: Whisper. Despite the gnawing doubt, despite the fear of another betrayal, Whisper was the only one who had shown a flicker of genuine concern, the only one who had hinted at the true horror of the Network's agenda. Whisper knew things, secrets buried deep within the organization. And Whisper, despite everything, had tried to help her escape.

The decision was a gamble, a desperate throw of the dice. Reaching Whisper meant exposing herself, risking capture or worse. But the alternative was a slow, inevitable suffocation in the tightening net. Anya had to believe that the desperation in Whisper's voice had been real, that the fear in her eyes hadn't been an act.

Finding Whisper would be like finding a ghost in a city of billions. She would have to rely on the fragmented knowledge Whisper had shared, the hidden communication channels, the unspoken codes. It would be a perilous journey, a step back into the heart of the beast. But with her face plastered across every street corner, with the hounds of both the Network and the Enforcers on her trail, Anya knew she had no other choice. Whisper was her only hope, a fragile lifeline in a city determined to swallow her whole. The hunted was now forced to seek out her hunter's shadow, praying that it held a flicker of salvation.

Chapter 33

Anya knew reaching Whisper was a near-impossible task. The Network's internal security was airtight, their communication channels encrypted beyond her current capabilities. Direct contact was suicide. She had to be subtle, to use the very systems that hunted her to send a ghost signal, a whisper in the digital static.

Remembering a fragmented piece of Network training – a contingency protocol for compromised operatives – Anya recalled a rarely used, low-frequency emergency broadcast system embedded within the city's ancient comms grid. It was designed for situations where standard channels were down, a digital whisper meant to be picked up by specific Network hardware using a unique decryption key.

The key, however, was the problem. Anya only remembered a partial sequence, a string of seemingly random alphanumeric characters Whisper had once muttered during a training exercise on emergency comms, emphasizing its absolute secrecy. It was a long shot, a desperate prayer sent into the void.

Finding a terminal old enough to access the low-frequency grid was a challenge in itself. Veridia had long since moved to more advanced systems. Anya finally located a relic in the depths of a forgotten tech repair shop in the Undercity, its screen flickering with archaic code. The shop owner, a wizened old cyborg with more wires than flesh, eyed her with suspicion but was more interested in the credits she offered than her face, which he hadn't bothered to properly scan.

Working quickly, Anya bypassed the terminal's outdated security, her fingers flying across the dusty keyboard. Accessing the low-frequency broadcast required a specific sequence, a digital handshake with the ancient system. Using the partial key she remembered, Anya began to cycle through variations, each attempt sending a silent ping into the city's hidden network.

Days blurred into nights as Anya tirelessly worked, fueled by scraps of synth-food and a desperate hope. The terminal was in a high-traffic area, forcing her to constantly watch her back, wary of both Enforcers and Network patrols. The risk of discovery was immense.

Just as her hope began to dwindle, a flicker on the terminal screen caught her eye. A brief, almost imperceptible acknowledgement – a single line of encrypted code that vanished as quickly as it appeared. It was a response. Someone had heard her whisper in the static.

Now came the even more dangerous part: establishing a secure channel. Anya knew the Network would be monitoring any unusual activity on these old frequencies. She needed a dead drop, a digital meeting point that couldn't be easily traced.

Remembering Whisper's fascination with ancient Veridian folklore, Anya recalled a specific urban legend – a ghost signal said to emanate from the deactivated Sky Gardens, a once-opulent aerial park now shrouded in decay and restricted airspace. It was a long shot, a place no one in their right mind would go.

Using the low-frequency terminal, Anya sent a single, encrypted message, embedding the partial key and a simple directive: *Sky Gardens. Observation Level Gamma. Sunrise.*

Then, she vanished back into the shadows, leaving the archaic terminal humming with its ghostly message. The risk was immense, her location potentially compromised. But the faint echo in the digital static offered a sliver of hope, a chance that Whisper, the only person who might hold the key to her survival and the truth, had heard her desperate plea. Now, all she could do was wait and pray that Whisper would risk everything to answer.

Chapter 34

The skeletal remains of the Sky Gardens clawed at the pre-dawn sky, their once vibrant flora now twisted metal and shattered synth-glass. A chilling wind whistled through the derelict structures, carrying the scent of rain and decay. Anya, hidden amongst the overgrown vines that snaked around a collapsed observation platform, shivered despite the rising sun painting the eastern horizon in hues of bruised purple and reluctant gold.

The wait had been agonizing, each rustle of leaves, each distant siren, sending a jolt of fear through her. The Sky Gardens were a forbidden zone, attracting unwanted attention from both Enforcer patrols and scavengers. Her vulnerability was amplified in the open, exposed to the early morning light.

Just as despair began to creep in, a flicker of movement caught her eye. A figure, cloaked and moving with a familiar, fluid grace, emerged from the shadows of a collapsed biodome. Whisper.

A wave of relief, so potent it almost buckled her knees, washed over Anya. Whisper had come.

But the relief was quickly tempered by a renewed surge of caution. Was this truly Whisper? Or a carefully orchestrated trap? Anya remained hidden, her senses on high alert, studying the approaching figure. The way she moved, the subtle tilt of her head, the almost imperceptible limp Anya had noticed during their training – it was Whisper.

Whisper's gaze swept across the ruined observation level, her cybernetic eyes scanning every shadow, every crevice. She moved with a tense alertness, her hand resting near the concealed sidearm Anya knew she carried. She was taking a considerable risk being here.

Finally, Whisper's gaze locked onto Anya's hiding place. A flicker of recognition, then a subtle nod, almost imperceptible to an outside observer.

Anya slowly emerged from the vines, her posture wary, her eyes fixed on Whisper. The distance between them felt vast, filled with unspoken accusations and the heavy weight of betrayal.

"Whisper," Anya said, her voice hoarse from disuse and suspicion.

Whisper didn't move, her expression unreadable in the dim light. "Anya. You shouldn't have come here." Her voice was low, strained.

"I had nowhere else to go," Anya replied, her gaze unwavering. "You said... you said what they were doing was worse than I could imagine. You said Silas was involved from the beginning."

A long silence stretched between them, broken only by the wind whistling through the ruins. Whisper finally nodded, a grim confirmation in her eyes. "It's true, Anya. Everything I said."

"Then why should I trust you?" Anya challenged, the bitterness in her voice palpable. "Everyone else... Silas, Cipher... the Network... they all lied."

Whisper took a slow step forward, her hands held open in a gesture of peace. "I know I haven't given you much reason to trust anyone, Anya. But believe me when I say, I was trying to protect you. To protect your mother's memory."

"Protect her memory?" Anya scoffed. "They took her! They're using her for whatever monstrous thing they're building!"

Tears welled in Whisper's eyes, a rare display of emotion that surprised Anya. "I tried to stop them, Anya. I tried. But Silas... he has too much influence. Cipher... he's blinded by ambition."

Whisper took another step closer, her voice dropping to a near whisper. "They're not just rewriting minds, Anya. They're merging consciousness, creating something... something unnatural. Your mother's unique neural structure... it was key to their initial breakthroughs. And your connection to the Spire device... they believe it can stabilize and amplify the process."

The horror of Whisper's words chilled Anya to the bone. Merging consciousness? Unnatural? Her mother, a key ingredient in this terrifying experiment?

"You need to understand, Anya," Whisper continued, her voice urgent. "Silas wasn't just involved in taking your mother. He was the one who identified her, who knew about her potential. He's been working with the organization behind Project Chimera for years, manipulating the Network from within."

The final piece of the puzzle clicked into place. Silas's unsettling interest in Anya's past, his subtle probing questions – it all made horrifying sense now.

"You have to believe me, Anya," Whisper pleaded, taking another step closer. "I want to help you stop them. To avenge your mother. But we have to do this together."

Anya stared at Whisper, searching her eyes for any hint of deceit. The desperation there felt genuine, the grief raw. The truth Whisper revealed was monstrous, confirming Anya's deepest fears.

Slowly, hesitantly, Anya lowered her guard. The isolation had been a suffocating burden, and the truth Whisper offered, however terrifying, provided a direction, a shared purpose.

"What do we do?" Anya asked, her voice barely a whisper. The fight had just become far more personal, and for the first time since going rogue, Anya didn't feel entirely alone. The serpent within the Network had been revealed, and the only way to strike back was with the help of another shadow.

Chapter 35

The fragile alliance forged in the ruins of the Sky Gardens propelled Anya and Whisper into the heart of the conspiracy. Whisper, now a trusted confidante, revealed hidden Network files and back channels, piecing together the horrifying truth about Project Chimera and the organization pulling its strings – a shadowy conglomerate known only as the Ascendant Collective.

Their trail led them through a labyrinth of clandestine research facilities and encrypted data vaults, each revelation more disturbing than the last. They learned the Ascendant Collective wasn't just merging consciousness; they were attempting to create a unified, controllable network of minds, believing it to be the next stage of human evolution – a terrifying vision of enforced unity. Anya's mother's unique neural architecture was indeed crucial to their early experiments, her resistance a key they sought to understand and overcome.

One clandestine data terminal, hidden deep within a decommissioned Enforcer archive, yielded a fragmented but vital clue. Amidst schematics detailing neural integration technology and lists of "candidate subjects," Anya's blood ran cold as she saw a familiar name: Misha Petrova. His designation was different, marked with a symbol indicating "potential integration nexus."

He wasn't just a missing person; he was a subject, possibly even a central component of the Ascendant Collective's horrifying project.

The same file contained a heavily redacted audio log. With Whisper's decryption skills, they managed to piece together a distorted voice – one Anya instantly recognized as her mother's. The recording was short, filled with static and pain, but one phrase cut through the noise like a shard of ice: "...they're taking him to the Spire... the central nexus..."

The Spire. The monolithic structure that dominated Veridia's skyline, the source of the ancient technology that now coursed through Anya's veins. It wasn't just a relic; it was the heart of the Ascendant Collective's operation, the central hub for their terrifying experiments.

A wave of conflicting emotions crashed over Anya – a surge of desperate hope that Misha was alive, a chilling fear of what they were doing to him, and a burning rage directed at the Ascendant Collective and their monstrous vision.

Whisper placed a comforting hand on Anya's arm, her expression grim. "The Spire... it's a fortress. We can't go in alone, not yet."

Anya looked at the towering structure dominating the horizon, a symbol of both ancient power and present horror. The clue had led them to her brother, but the sheer scale of the Ascendant Collective's operation within the Spire felt overwhelming. They were just two against a force that had infiltrated the Network and was now attempting to reshape humanity itself.

"You're right," Anya conceded, a reluctant understanding dawning within her. Rushing in blindly would be suicide. They needed a different approach, a way to level the playing field.

Whisper nodded, her cybernetic eyes gleaming with a spark of a new plan. "There are others, Anya. Others who have seen the Ascendant Collective's true face, who have suffered under their influence. Disillusioned Network operatives, former scientists, those the Collective deemed... unsuitable for integration."

A flicker of hope ignited within Anya. They weren't alone in this fight. The Ascendant Collective's ambition likely left a trail of broken lives and simmering resentment.

"We find them," Anya said, a newfound determination hardening her gaze. "We find those who have been hurt, those who want to fight back."

Whisper smiled, a rare but genuine expression of hope. "It won't be easy. They'll be scattered, hiding in the shadows, just like us. But they're out there. And with your connection to the Spire technology, Anya... it might resonate with others who possess similar, latent abilities. We could be the spark that ignites a rebellion."

Turning their backs on the imposing silhouette of the Spire for now, Anya and Whisper melted back into the city's underbelly. The clue about Misha was a painful beacon, a promise of a future confrontation. But they knew their immediate task was to gather strength, to find others who would stand against the Ascendant Collective's terrifying vision. The fight for Anya's family, and for the soul of Veridia, was far from over. It was just beginning, with two figures disappearing into the neon shadows, carrying the first seeds of a desperate rebellion.

Chapter 36

The weight of the Network's ambition pressed down on Veridia, a suffocating shroud woven from lies and control. Anya and Whisper, bound by a shared enemy and a desperate hope, knew they couldn't fight this war alone. The Spire loomed, a symbol of the Network's pervasive power, and their plan shifted from immediate destruction to the more intricate and perilous task of building an army in the shadows.

"We can't just go loud, Anya," Whisper said, holographic schematics of the Spire shimmering between them. "A city-wide blackout... it's a last resort. It would hurt everyone, including those we might want to help."

Anya, her gaze still drawn to the Spire's imposing silhouette, nodded slowly. The raw desire for immediate action warred with a growing understanding of the need for a more strategic approach. "So we find others. Those who have been hurt, those who see what the Network is doing."

Whisper's cybernetic eyes gleamed with a spark of a plan. "They're out there. Disillusioned Network operatives who couldn't stomach Silas's rise, former Network scientists who witnessed the early, brutal stages of Project Chimera, even those living in the Undercity who've seen their neighbors disappear without a trace – all thanks to the Network's 'greater good'."

CHAPTER 36

Their focus shifted from immediate sabotage to recruitment. The power substation became their makeshift headquarters, a nexus for whispered communications and clandestine meetings. Whisper's network, built over years of navigating Veridia's undercurrents and exploiting the Network's own internal divisions, became their primary tool. She reached out to her contacts, sending coded messages through encrypted channels, seeking individuals with specific skills and a burning desire for change.

"We need eyes and ears, Anya," Whisper explained, her fingers flying across a holographic interface displaying a web of potential allies. "Hackers who can breach the Network's firewalls, fighters who can hold their own against their enforcers, medics who understand neural pathways... and most importantly, people who have lost something because of the Network."

Anya's own experience became a powerful recruiting tool. Her story – the Network's betrayal, her mother and brother's abduction, the horrifying glimpse into Project Chimera – resonated with those who had their own scars from the organization's ruthless efficiency. The Spire device, though a risk, also served as a subtle identifier, a shared anomaly that drew certain individuals to their cause – those who had witnessed or been affected by the Network's more esoteric projects.

Their initial recruits were a motley crew: a former Network data analyst haunted by the redacted files he had processed, a brilliant but ostracized Network bio-engineer with intimate knowledge of Project Chimera's early research, and a hardened Undercity enforcer whose family had vanished after questioning the Network's activities in their sector. Each brought unique skills and a shared thirst for justice against the very organization they had once served or feared.

The planning sessions evolved. Instead of immediate destruction, they began to strategize smaller, targeted strikes: disrupting Network supply lines, rescuing potential Project Chimera subjects held in secret facilities, leaking damaging information into the public net to sow seeds of doubt and fear about the Network's true agenda.

"We need to show Veridia what the Network is really doing, Anya," Whisper emphasized. "We need to wake people up before they become willing sacrifices to their 'greater good'."

Recruiting was a delicate dance, requiring trust and discretion in a city saturated with Network surveillance. Anya and Whisper learned to read the subtle tells, the flicker of anger in someone's eyes, the barely suppressed grief in their voice – all directed at the Network. They offered not just a chance for revenge, but a purpose, a way to fight back against a seemingly insurmountable enemy that had its tendrils wrapped around every aspect of Veridian life.

The power substation, once a symbol of forgotten infrastructure, began to hum with a different kind of energy – the nascent power of a growing rebellion against the Network. Anya and Whisper, no longer just fugitives, were becoming leaders, forging a shadow syndicate united by loss and a shared determination to dismantle the Network's terrifying reign. The path ahead was fraught with peril, but for the first time since going rogue, Anya felt a flicker of hope, not just for her family, but for the soul of Veridia itself, as they gathered those brave enough to stand against the all-powerful Network.

Chapter 37

Months had passed since Anya and Whisper formed their shadow syndicate. The power substation, now a bustling hub of clandestine activity, pulsed with a nervous energy. Their ranks had swelled, a motley crew united by a shared hatred of the Network and a desperate hope for a better Veridia. They had become a thorn in the Network's side, disrupting supply lines, leaking sensitive information, and rescuing those targeted for Project Chimera.

Their most ambitious operation to date was targeting a Network "donor" delivery. Intel, gleaned from a disillusioned Network medic, indicated a shipment of individuals being transported to a remote research facility on the city's outskirts. This facility, known as the "Chrysalis," was rumored to be a testing ground for advanced integration techniques.

The ambush was swift and brutal. Anya, leading a strike team composed of hardened Undercity enforcers and former Network operatives, intercepted the heavily armored transport convoy on a deserted stretch of highway. The fighting was fierce, the Network's security forces well-equipped and ruthless. But Anya's team, fueled by a burning desire for retribution, fought with a desperate ferocity.

As the dust settled and the last Network enforcer fell, Anya moved to secure the transport's cargo hold. What she found inside sent a jolt of disbelief through her. Huddled in the cramped space, their faces gaunt and their eyes filled with fear, were the intended "donors." But among them, strapped to a medical gurney, was a figure that made Anya's blood run cold.

Griffin.

His face was pale, his body weakened, but there was no mistaking the familiar features. He was alive. The Network hadn't killed him. They had kept him, a prisoner, likely a subject for Project Chimera.

"Griffin," Anya breathed, reaching for him.

But before she could reach the restraints, a high-pitched whine filled the air. From the direction the convoy had come, sleek, black vehicles bearing no Network markings screeched to a halt. Figures in sterile white suits, their faces obscured by featureless helmets, emerged with unsettling speed and efficiency.

"Asset retrieval initiated," a synthesized voice echoed from their ranks.

Anya and her team reacted instantly, raising their weapons. But these newcomers moved with a chilling precision, their energy weapons emitting a familiar, faint blue glow — a resonance that sent a shiver down Anya's spine. It was similar, eerily similar, to the energy signature of her own Spire device. A brief, chaotic firefight erupted. Anya fought with a renewed fury, desperate to protect Griffin.

But these forces were overwhelming. They moved with a disturbing coordination, their tactics flawless. Before Anya could reach Griffin, two of them efficiently detached his gurney and retreated towards their vehicles.

"No!" Anya roared, lunging forward. But a searing energy

CHAPTER 37

blast, the same unsettling blue, slammed into her shoulder, sending her sprawling.

Whisper, pulling Anya back, her face grim, said, "We can't win this fight, Anya. They're not standard Network. Their tech... it's like yours, but... refined."

By the time Anya and her team regrouped, the black vehicles had vanished, leaving behind only the smoldering wreckage of the Network transport and the bitter taste of a victory turned to ash. Griffin was gone, snatched away by a force operating with technology akin to her own.

Back at the substation, the initial elation had been replaced by a heavy, oppressive silence. Griffin was alive, but now he was in the hands of an even more dangerous enemy.

"Those weapons..." Anya said, her voice tight with a mixture of confusion and dread. "That energy... it was like the Spire device."

Whisper's cybernetic eyes narrowed in thought. "The Network... they must have found something. Something similar to your chip. A source, or perhaps even another working device."

A chilling realization settled over the group. The Network wasn't just ruthless; they were evolving, gaining access to technology that mirrored Anya's own unique power. And they had Griffin.

"We have to get him back," Anya said, her voice raw with a renewed sense of urgency. The guilt she felt for leaving him in the Foundry now burned hotter than ever. This time, she wouldn't fail him.

The planning began anew, the schematics of the Chrysalis now viewed through a lens of terrifying uncertainty. The Network had leveled the playing field in a way they hadn't anticipated. The rescue of Griffin was no longer just about saving a friend; it was about facing a Network armed with a dangerous new power, a power that echoed the very source of Anya's strength. The fight had just become a whole lot more complicated.

Chapter 38

The Chrysalis loomed on the horizon, a sterile white complex against the bruised twilight sky. Infiltrating the Network facility was a far riskier proposition than their previous operations. The capture of Griffin, and the Network's deployment of Spire-like technology during the snatch, had put them on high alert. Security was tighter, patrols more frequent, and the air hummed with an unsettling energy.

Anya's team, a smaller, more specialized unit led by her and Whisper, moved through the facility's outer perimeter under the cover of a manufactured electromagnetic pulse, a temporary blind spot created by their tech expert, a jittery former Network engineer named Jax.

The inside was a labyrinth of sterile corridors and locked doors. Whisper's network of informants had provided them with partial schematics, but the Network had clearly upgraded its security systems. Every turn held the potential for a lethal encounter.

Their objective was Griffin's last known location – a Level 5 research lab deep within the complex. The intel suggested he was being subjected to intense experimentation related to Project Chimera and, chillingly, the Network's attempts to replicate or understand Anya's Spire device.

They encountered resistance – heavily armed Network enforcers wielding energy weapons with that familiar blue resonance. Anya fought with a desperate ferocity, her hand hovering near her pouch, where the Spire device pulsed with a restrained energy. She had been hesitant to use it, fearing detection by the Network's own similar technology. But the closer they got to Griffin, the more desperate the situation became.

Reaching a heavily fortified blast door guarding Level 5, they were met by Silas. His face was a mask of cold fury, his eyes glinting with a newfound confidence. He held a device in his hand, small and intricate, emitting the same faint blue light as Anya's.

"Anya," Silas sneered, his voice amplified through the corridor's comm system. "I knew you'd come crawling back. But you're too late. We've unlocked the secrets of your little toy. And soon, its power will be ours."

A fierce battle ensued. Silas, wielding his own Spire-derived technology, was a formidable opponent, his attacks mirroring Anya's potential abilities. Her team fought valiantly, but they were outmatched by Silas and the enhanced security forces he commanded.

Cornered and with her team taking heavy fire, Anya knew she had no choice. Griffin's life hung in the balance. With a deep breath, she drew the Spire device from her pouch. The familiar warmth spread through her veins as it activated, her senses sharpening, her reflexes accelerating. The air around her crackled with energy.

The effect was immediate. The blue energy emanating from her device clashed with Silas's, creating a volatile feedback loop. Anya moved with a speed the Network operatives couldn't track, her strikes precise and devastating. The world seemed to slow around her, the flow of time bending to her will.

Silas, surprised by the raw power of Anya's connection, staggered back. His own device sputtered, unable to handle the resonance. Anya pressed her advantage, her focus solely on reaching Griffin.

She found him in a sterile chamber, strapped to a table, wires snaking from his head. Network scientists in white coats frantically worked at consoles, their faces illuminated by flickering monitors displaying complex neural patterns.

Ignoring the scientists, Anya unleashed a focused pulse of energy from her device, targeting the restraints holding Griffin. The metal hissed and melted away.

But the surge of power had a cost. The Network's internal sensors went haywire, alarms blaring throughout the facility. Their location was compromised. And Silas, recovering from the initial shock, was rallying his forces.

Anya grabbed Griffin, his body weak and unresponsive. "Whisper! We need to get out of here!"

Their escape was chaotic, a desperate sprint through the labyrinthine facility with the entire Network security force on their tail. Anya, fueled by the Spire device, created diversions, overloaded circuits, and moved with superhuman speed, carrying Griffin's weight.

They reached their extraction point, a hidden access tunnel leading back to the outside. As they burst into the night air, Silas and a contingent of heavily armed operatives were close behind.

Anya knew they couldn't outrun them. Turning to face her pursuers, the Spire device pulsed brightly in her hand. The price of saving Griffin had been the full, uncontrolled unleashing of her power, a power that had now painted a massive target on her back. The Network knew what she could do, and they would hunt her relentlessly. But as she looked down at Griffin's unconscious face, a fierce determination hardened her gaze. She had made her choice. The fight had just entered a dangerous new phase.

Chapter 39

The piercing shriek of alarms echoed through the Chrysalis, a frantic symphony accompanying Anya's desperate escape with the weakened Griffin in her arms. Whisper and Jax, their faces grim, covered their retreat, firing bursts of scavenged energy weapons at the pursuing Network operatives.

"Go, Anya! We'll hold them!" Whisper yelled over the din, her form a blur of motion as she disabled a security drone with a well-aimed shot.

Jax, his hands flying across a handheld device, muttered, "Almost there… almost there…"

They reached the extraction point – a maintenance tunnel leading to the surface. As Anya squeezed through the narrow opening, a deafening roar ripped through the facility. The ground beneath her feet bucked violently.

"What was that?" Anya gasped, stumbling forward with Griffin.

From the tunnel entrance, Jax's voice crackled with a grim satisfaction. "Insurance. Figured if we were going down, they were coming with us."

Anya didn't need to ask what he meant. The sheer force of the explosion shook the very foundations of the Chrysalis. Twisted metal groaned, and chunks of the building began to shear away.

The tower, once a symbol of the Network's insidious ambition, was tearing itself apart.

"We need to move! Now!" Whisper yelled, pulling Anya further into the tunnel. The air was thick with dust and the smell of burning circuitry. The sounds of collapsing structures echoed around them.

Their escape through the narrow, debris-filled tunnel was a harrowing race against time. The Chrysalis was a dying beast, its metal bones groaning under immense stress. Anya, fueled by adrenaline and the desperate need to protect Griffin, pushed forward, ignoring the searing pain in her shoulder.

They finally burst out into the night air, the sight of the collapsing Chrysalis a terrifying spectacle. Flames licked at the fractured structure, and sections of the tower plummeted to the ground in fiery cascades.

Waiting for them was a heavily modified transport vehicle, piloted by a hulking former Network driver named Boris. "Get in! We're on a tight schedule!" he roared over the cacophony.

Whisper and Jax clambered aboard, helping Anya settle Griffin onto a makeshift medical bed in the back. As Boris gunned the engine, the transport lurched forward, speeding away from the crumbling facility.

Looking back, Anya watched in grim satisfaction as the Chrysalis continued its violent descent, a monument to the Network's shattered secrets. Griffin was safe, extracted from their clutches. A small victory amidst the chaos.

But as they sped away, a large section of the collapsing tower shifted unexpectedly. A shockwave rippled outwards, catching their transport in its violent wake. The vehicle swerved violently, throwing Anya against the bulkhead.

Through the dust-filled air, Anya saw a massive chunk of the

CHAPTER 39

Chrysalis plummeting directly towards their escape route. Boris fought desperately with the controls, but it was too late.

The transport was engulfed in a shower of debris and the force of the impact threw Anya forward. The last thing she saw was Whisper's horrified face before darkness claimed her as the world around her dissolved into a maelstrom of falling steel and concrete. Griffin was safe, she had made sure of that. But Anya Petrova was trapped within the tower's death throes.

Chapter 40

The world dissolved into a violent cacophony of screeching metal, shattering concrete, and the deafening roar of the Chrysalis tearing itself apart. Anya, thrown against the transport's bulkhead, fought to regain her senses, her head swimming in a haze of pain and disorientation. Dust and debris rained down, filling the air and choking her lungs.

Through the swirling chaos, she could vaguely hear Whisper's frantic shouts and the groan of stressed metal as the transport bucked violently. But her focus was drawn back to the collapsing tower, its fractured silhouette a terrifying dance against the night sky.

A primal instinct for survival surged through Anya. Griffin was safe, she had ensured that. But she was still within the tower's deadly embrace, trapped in a metal coffin rapidly descending towards the ground.

Ignoring the throbbing pain in her head and shoulder, Anya scrambled to her feet, her vision still blurred. The transport, though damaged, was still somewhat intact, wedged amidst a pile of debris. But the structure around them was giving way with terrifying speed.

"Whisper! Jax! Boris!" she yelled, her voice barely audible above the din. There was no response, only the relentless

CHAPTER 40

groaning of the collapsing building.

Anya knew she couldn't wait. The transport wouldn't hold for long. She had to find a way out, a path through the falling debris and twisted metal.

Activating the Spire device, she focused her senses, trying to perceive the shifting structure around her, searching for a pocket of relative safety, a potential escape route. The device pulsed with a frantic energy, its output erratic amidst the surrounding chaos.

The floor beneath her feet tilted sharply as another section of the tower gave way. Anya stumbled, grabbing onto a mangled support beam to keep from falling. The air grew hotter, the smell of burning fuel acrid in her nostrils.

She spotted a narrow shaft, a ventilation duct ripped open by the collapse, offering a precarious climb upwards. It was a long shot, a claustrophobic passage through the building's dying innards, but it was her only option.

With grim determination, Anya began to climb, her injured shoulder screaming in protest. Jagged edges of metal tore at her clothes, and the constant tremors threatened to throw her from her precarious handholds. Above her, the shaft was intermittently illuminated by flashes of fire and falling debris.

The tower groaned again, a deep, guttural sound that vibrated through her bones. The ventilation shaft shifted violently, and a shower of smaller debris rained down on her. Anya pressed herself against the metal walls, shielding her head.

Just as she thought she might reach a higher level, a massive section of the ceiling above her buckled and crashed down, blocking her ascent. The force of the impact sent a shockwave through the shaft, throwing Anya against the metal.

A sharp pain lanced through her skull as her head collided

with the unforgiving steel. Her grip loosened, and for a terrifying moment, she dangled precariously in the darkness. She managed to regain her hold, her knuckles white against the metal.

But the impact had taken its toll. A wave of dizziness washed over her, and her vision swam. The relentless shaking of the collapsing building, the lack of air, the searing pain – it was all too much.

Her grip weakened again, her fingers slipping. The last thing Anya saw, before the darkness finally claimed her, was the distorted image of the falling debris above, the crumbling tower claiming another victim in its violent demise.

Chapter 41

Anya drifted in a black void, punctuated by fleeting flickers of sensation. A jarring lurch, the rough texture of fabric against her skin, the distant hum of machinery. Then, oblivion again.

The darkness would recede momentarily, replaced by a kaleidoscope of blurred shapes and muffled sounds. She glimpsed a figure looming above her, their face obscured by shadow, their arms supporting her weight. A sense of motion, a smooth gliding sensation, as if she were being carried. Then, the blackness would return, a merciful blanket against the pain that throbbed in her head.

The cycle repeated, each return to awareness bringing her closer to a coherent reality. The humming grew louder, more persistent. The feeling of motion ceased. She felt a cold, hard surface beneath her, the scent of antiseptic stinging her nostrils.

Her eyelids fluttered open, heavy and resistant. The light was harsh, sterile white, making her wince. Her vision swam, resolving slowly into the blurry shapes of a room. Walls lined with gleaming metal, complex machinery blinking with an array of lights, and figures moving with quiet efficiency. A lab. She was in a lab.

A face swam into focus above her – Silas. His features were sharp, his expression unreadable, though a hint of something akin to... triumph?... flickered in his eyes. He was speaking, his lips moving, but the sounds that reached Anya were distorted, muffled, as if she were underwater. She strained to understand, to grasp the meaning of his words, but they remained a meaningless jumble.

Panic began to claw at the edges of her consciousness. Where was she? What had happened? Griffin... was he safe? The memory of the tower's collapse, the crushing darkness... it sent a fresh wave of pain through her head.

Another figure approached, stepping into Silas's shadow. This one wore a white lab coat, their face partially obscured by a surgical mask. They leaned closer, their voice soft, soothing. They were speaking to her, their tone gentle, but again, the words were incomprehensible, a comforting murmur that held no meaning.

A hand, gloved and cool, touched her forehead. Anya flinched, her body tensing despite its leaden weight. She tried to speak, to ask about Griffin, to demand answers, but only a strangled groan escaped her lips. Her thoughts were sluggish, her mind a fog. She couldn't focus, couldn't understand. She was trapped in a silent, incomprehensible nightmare, held captive in this sterile white prison, with the last coherent image being the crumbling tower and the encroaching darkness. The world around her was a distorted puzzle, and she was lost within its fragmented reality.

Chapter 42

The fog in Anya's mind finally began to dissipate, the edges of reality sharpening with a painful clarity. She blinked, her eyes adjusting to the relentless glare of the overhead lights. Awareness flooded back, bringing with it the throbbing ache in her head, the dull throb in her shoulder, and the chilling memory of the tower's violent demise.

She was lying on a narrow medical bed, her limbs heavy and unresponsive. Panic flared as she tried to move, to push herself up, but found her wrists and ankles securely fastened by thick, reinforced straps. Cold metal bit into her skin. She was completely immobilized.

Fear turned to a cold dread as she took in her surroundings. The lab was even more sterile and foreboding in full awareness. Gleaming instruments lined metal trays, monitors flickered with incomprehensible data streams, and the air hummed with the constant thrum of unseen machinery. Network personnel in white coats moved with a detached efficiency, their faces impassive as they went about their tasks.

Anya tried to speak, to call out for Whisper, for Griffin, but her throat was dry and her voice a weak croak. Her mind raced, piecing together the fragmented memories: the tower falling, the darkness, being carried… they had found her. The Network had found her.

A figure approached her bed – the scientist who had tried to calm her earlier. This time, their words were clear, though their tone remained clinical. "Subject is regaining consciousness. Initiate Phase Two diagnostics."

Phase Two. The words sent a fresh wave of terror through Anya. She was a specimen, an experiment.

The scientist gestured, and two other personnel approached, wheeling over a complex array of scanning equipment. Cold probes were pressed against her temples, and a helmet-like device was lowered over her head. The monitors beside her bed sprang to life, displaying intricate patterns of neural activity.

A wave of nausea washed over Anya as the scanning began. It felt invasive, violating, as if they were picking through her thoughts, mapping the very essence of her being. She squeezed her eyes shut, trying to block out the sensation, the cold, impersonal touch of their technology.

Then, they turned their attention to the Spire device. Carefully, reverently, a technician approached her pouch and extracted it. The faint blue light pulsed steadily in the sterile environment. They placed it on a shielded platform, and a battery of sensors descended upon it, analyzing its energy signature, its composition, its every minute detail.

Anya watched, helpless, as they examined the source of her power, the key to her connection. They were dissecting it, trying to understand it, to replicate it, just as Silas had hinted.

Silas himself appeared, observing the tests with a cold satisfaction. He didn't speak directly to Anya, but his gaze lingered on her, a predatory gleam in his eyes. He gestured towards the Spire device, then back at Anya, as if making a silent connection, a possessive claim.

CHAPTER 42

Helpless and restrained, Anya could only watch as they probed her mind and analyzed the device that had become a part of her. She was trapped, a prisoner in their sterile lab, her unique connection a subject of intense scrutiny. The fight for Griffin had cost her dearly, and now she was at their mercy, a pawn in their terrifying game. The price of her power had become her captivity.

Chapter 43

The tests continued for what felt like an eternity, invasive and dehumanizing. Anya remained strapped to the cold medical bed, a powerless subject under the Network's relentless scrutiny. Finally, the scientists withdrew their instruments, their expressions unreadable. Silas approached, his usual cold demeanor tinged with a calculated softness.

"Anya," he said, his voice surprisingly gentle, a stark contrast to his previous sneers. "Rest. You've been through a great deal."

Anya glared at him, her eyes narrowed with hatred. "Where are they? Griffin? Whisper?" Her voice was still hoarse, but the defiance was clear.

Silas offered a small, almost pitying smile. "Griffin is... being cared for. As for Whisper... her concern for you was... noted." He let the implication hang in the air.

Then, his tone shifted, becoming more persuasive. "But I want to talk about your family, Anya. Your mother. Your brother, Misha."

A jolt of fear shot through Anya. "What have you done to them?"

Silas gestured to a nearby screen, and a series of images flickered to life. Anya's breath caught in her throat. There was her mother, Elena, looking pale but stable, engaged in what appeared to be a neurological examination. Another image showed Misha, lying in a similar medical bed, his eyes closed, but seemingly unharmed. A wave of relief washed over Anya, quickly followed by a surge of suspicion.

"They are safe, Anya," Silas said, watching her reaction intently. "Under our care. We understand their... unique value."

"You're lying," Anya spat, straining against the restraints. "You took them. You're using them for Project Chimera!"

Silas sighed, a theatrical display of weariness. "Project Chimera is about the future, Anya. A future where humanity transcends its limitations. Your family... they possess certain... affinities that are crucial to our understanding."

He leaned closer, his voice dropping to a conspiratorial whisper. "But this doesn't have to be their fate. Or yours."

He gestured to the Spire device, still humming softly on its shielded platform. "This... this bond you share. It's the key, Anya. It's what makes you... special. And it's what makes you a threat."

"A threat to what? Your twisted idea of progress?" Anya retorted, her voice laced with scorn.

Silas ignored her defiance. "We can offer you a different path. Cooperation. If you willingly relinquish your bond to the device, if you allow us to study its connection to you... then your family will be released. Safe. Untouched."

Anya stared at him, her mind racing. It was a tempting offer, a chance to secure her mother and brother's freedom. But the look in Silas's eyes, the cold calculation beneath his veneer of reason, filled her with distrust.

"I don't believe you," she said, her voice firm despite the tremor of hope that had flickered within her. "You'd never let them go. You'd just find another way to use them."

Silas's smile faded, replaced by a hint of steel. "You underestimate our commitment to the project, Anya. And you overestimate your own importance. The device... it's the key. You are merely the lock."

He paused, letting his words sink in. "Think about it, Anya. Their safety... your freedom. All you have to do is cooperate." He turned and walked towards the door, his final words hanging in the sterile air. "The offer stands. For now."

Anya was left alone, strapped to the bed, the images of her mother and brother burned into her mind. A terrible choice lay before her, a bargain offered by the very serpent who had orchestrated her family's suffering. Could she trust him? Could she risk their lives on his empty promises? The Spire device pulsed faintly nearby, a silent reminder of the power that both bound and threatened to tear her family apart. The serpent's bargain had been struck, and Anya Petrova was caught in its venomous coils.

Chapter 44

Silas watched the data streams scrolling across the monitors, his brow furrowed in frustration. The Spire device, even under the Network's most advanced analysis, remained stubbornly enigmatic. Its energy signature defied conventional physics, its composition hinted at technologies far beyond their current understanding.

Dr. Aris Thorne, the lead scientist on the project, approached Silas, his face etched with a mixture of fascination and exasperation. "Director, the initial diagnostics are complete. However, the device's nature is... unusual. Its energy fluctuations are unlike anything we've encountered. The bio-integration with the subject, Petrova, is equally perplexing. It's not a simple symbiotic relationship; it's far more intricate, almost... interwoven at a fundamental level."

Silas turned, his impatience barely concealed. "So, what are you saying, Doctor? Can we replicate it? Can we sever Petrova's connection and harness its power for Project Chimera?"

Thorne shook his head slowly. "Director, I can't give you a definitive timeline. Understanding the device's principles, let alone replicating them or safely severing its bond with Petrova... it will take time. Significant time. Its very origin seems to defy our current scientific paradigms. We're charting unknown territory here."

Silas's jaw tightened. Time was a luxury they couldn't afford. The near-collapse of the Chrysalis had been a setback, a glaring vulnerability exposed by Petrova and her ragtag group. He needed the power of the Spire device, or at least an understanding of it, to secure their dominance and accelerate Project Chimera.

He turned back to the shielded platform where the device pulsed with its mysterious blue light. "Its origin..." he murmured aloud, more to himself than to Thorne. "Where did Petrova find it? It's unlike anything I've ever encountered in Network archives or intelligence."

Thorne shrugged, adjusting his glasses. "The subject's file indicates she discovered it during a scavenging run in the Serpent's Coil, Director. A derelict section rumored to contain pre-Network artifacts. We dismissed it as low priority at the time."

Silas's eyes narrowed. Pre-Network artifacts. The Serpent's Coil was a chaotic graveyard of forgotten technology, remnants of Veridia's long and often turbulent history. Could this device be a relic from a lost era, a power source beyond their current comprehension?

"Investigate," Silas ordered, his voice sharp. "Divert resources. I want every record, every rumor, every scrap of information about pre-Network technology in the Serpent's Coil. Focus on anything related to energy sources or neural interfaces. Petrova stumbled upon something significant, Doctor. Something that could hold the key to Project Chimera's success... or our downfall if we don't understand it."

He turned back to the restrained Anya, her defiant gaze fixed on him. She was more than just a subject; she was a living link to an unknown power. And Silas was determined to unravel the mystery of its origin, even if it meant delving into the forgotten depths of Veridia's past. The enigma of the Spire device, and its connection to Anya Petrova, had become his new obsession.

Chapter 45

Days bled into weeks within the sterile confines of the Network lab. Anya remained a prisoner, subjected to relentless tests and Silas's increasingly insistent demands for cooperation. The weight of her captivity, the uncertainty surrounding Griffin and Whisper, and the chilling realization of the Network's interest in the Spire device pressed down on her.

During one particularly invasive neural scan, a terrifying thought sparked in Anya's mind. If the Network could analyze and potentially replicate the Spire device's energy signature, and if they had managed to track *her* through its unique resonance, then perhaps there were others like her, individuals connected to similar artifacts scattered throughout Veridia's forgotten corners.

The Serpent's Coil, the pre-Network ruins... Thorne's words echoed in her memory. If her device was a relic, a piece of a lost technology, then the chances of other such relics existing were not insignificant. And if the Network could track one, they could potentially track them all, turning anyone with a similar connection into a target for Project Chimera.

A cold dread washed over Anya. She wasn't just fighting for herself and her immediate allies; she could be unknowingly endangering others, individuals with dormant power waiting to be discovered and exploited by the Network.

A small, grim satisfaction bloomed within her. At least she had ensured one thing. During her escape from the Chrysalis, in the chaos of the tower's collapse, she had instinctively reacted when she sensed a Network operative attempting to tag her with a small, metallic tracker – a device emitting a faint energy signature designed to lock onto the Spire device's resonance. With a surge of power, fueled by adrenaline and the collapsing structure around her, she had crushed it under her boot, the faint blue glow dissipating into nothingness.

They wouldn't be able to track *her* device easily. That small act of defiance, a fleeting moment amidst the destruction, now felt like a crucial victory. It bought her time, and perhaps, unknowingly, protected others who might share her connection.

Lying strapped to the cold bed, Anya's gaze hardened. Silas's offer of freedom for her family in exchange for her cooperation was a lie, she knew it in her bones. But the realization that her device could be a key to finding others, and the knowledge that she had at least destroyed their immediate means of tracking her specific resonance, sparked a new kind of hope.

Her captivity wouldn't be in vain. She would endure their tests, their manipulations, and she would use every moment to understand their methods, to find a weakness in their system. Because now, her fight wasn't just personal. It was about protecting a potential network of others, hidden echoes of a forgotten power, waiting to be awakened in the shadows of Veridia. The game had changed. Anya Petrova was a prisoner, but she was also a potential catalyst, and the resonance of her defiance was just beginning to be felt.

About The Author

Tristyn Barberi is a serving member of the United States Navy who has embarked on a new and exciting adventure: the world of writing. Finding joy and creative expression in crafting stories, Tristyn approaches authorship with the same dedication and discipline honed through naval service. While navigating the demands of military life, Tristyn carves out time to explore imaginative landscapes and bring compelling characters to life, writing purely for the love of it.

Also By Tristyn Barberi

-Neon Shadows
City Of Whispers
City Of Sorrow

www.ingramcontent.com/pod-product-compliance
Lightning Source LLC
LaVergne TN
LVHW092049060526
838201LV00047B/1306